TORPEDO TREASURE

*Depth Force Thrillers
Book Fourteen*

Irving A Greenfield

TORPEDO TREASURE

Published by Sapere Books.

24 Trafalgar Road, Ilkley, LS29 8HH,
United Kingdom

saperebooks.com

Copyright © Irving A Greenfield, 1991

Irving A Greenfield has asserted his right to be identified as
the author of this work.
All rights reserved.

No part of this publication may be reproduced, stored in any retrieval system, or transmitted, in any form, or by any means, electronic, mechanical, photocopying, recording, or otherwise, without the prior written permission of the publishers.
This book is a work of fiction. Names, characters, businesses, organisations, places and events, other than those clearly in the public domain, are either the product of the author's imagination, or are used fictitiously.
Any resemblances to actual persons, living or dead, events or locales are purely coincidental.

ISBN: 978-0-85495-017-1

TORPEDO ATTACK!

"Load all four forward tubes," Boxer said, riding the periscope up and turning it in the direction of the enemy vessels. "They're fanned out... Come to course two-five-zero."

"I have the helm," Stark said. "Coming to course two-five-zero."

"Six thousands yards and closing fast!"

The U-69 positioned at a ninety-degree intercept course with their target, Boxer ordered all engines stopped.

"Stand by ... fire one and two!" Boxer barked.

A hissing sound filled the submarine, and it rose slightly.

"One and two away, sir!"

Boxer watched through the periscope as the first enemy ship started to turn away from the torpedo's course. Too late by a second, the ship exploded into a ball of orange flame upon impact.

"Take her down, Mr. Stark... Now!"

CHAPTER 1

Boxer looked up at incredibly blue sky partially curtained by the *Sea Dog*'s foresail and lined by the ketch's rigging. He listened to the gentle swish of the water as the ship's bow sliced through the water of the South China Sea.

This was a part of the world's oceans that he had never sailed, but his good friend, the former Chief of Naval Operations, who now had the conn, had made several submarine patrols in the area during World War II, when he was a submariner.

Boxer too had been a submariner, and technically still was. But after his last assignment and his problems with the several people in and out of the Navy, he had decided to take a leave of absence. And in the old-fashion sense, follow his star. He and Stark decided to do what most men dream about doing: they bought the *Sea Dog*, a Dutch double ender, equipped it with sophisticated radar and radio gear, even a high-tech, three-dimensional display fathometer, and started to sail around the world.

If necessary, the *Sea Dog* could be worked by just the two of them, but more often than not it was crewed by their friends, who were more than willing to fly thousands of miles to spend a few restful days at sea with them.

Boxer had three guests aboard on this leg of their voyage that had begun three days before in Manila and would end in Hong Kong, still another three to four days away.

One of the shipboard guests was Boxer's longtime friend, Navy Captain Pepe Paskudnyak, whose lineage could be traced back to the Jews who were forced to leave Spain because of the Inquisition. Pepe, a tall, rangy man, was also a submariner, and commanded the nuclear attack boat *Barracuda*. Like Boxer, Pepe had a number of women in his life. He brought his latest interest, Odah Barhoop, a Lebanese beauty of twenty-five or so, with him from the States.

The other guest on board was the woman lying next to Boxer, Dr. Louise Decena, an exquisite Amerasian whom he had met at a cocktail party in Manila just four days before.

Boxer lowered his gaze, shifted his head, and looked at Louise, whose svelte, almost-naked body was very tan, and who, to his surprise, was just as frankly appraising him as he was appraising her.

For an instant they stared at one another, then, simultaneously, they began to smile and, finally, guffaw.

"Now, you tell me what you were thinking about," Louise said, "and I'll tell you what I was thinking about."

"I was thinking that I was a very lucky man to be in the company of such a beautiful woman," Boxer answered.

"Ah, flattery will get you everywhere," she answered.

"Your turn," Boxer said.

"That I must have been mad to agree to accompany you," she told him with a smile.

"Is that all?"

"Isn't that enough? Here I am, a respectable staff member of the International Hospital, on a boat with a man I hardly know, when I should be hard at work —"

Boxer held up his hand.

"What's wrong?" she asked.

"Where is it written in stone, or any other material, that you should be hard at work?" Boxer asked.

She laughed. "Haven't you ever worked?"

"Not if I could help it," Boxer answered. He had told her nothing about his past activities, or that he still held the rank of admiral. To her, and to the other woman aboard, he and Stark were just two men who happened to have enough money to do exactly what they wanted, which happened to be absolutely true. Both were millionaires several times over.

"Ah, for the life of the idle rich," she commented with mock longing.

"It's not a bad life. You ought to try it sometime," Boxer responded.

"That's why I'm here, I think," she said.

"I'm deeply wounded," he told her.

She raised her eyebrows.

"I thought you were here because you found me sexually irresistible," Boxer told her.

She held out her hand and rocked it from side to side. "Sixty-forty."

"Sixty for being sexually —"

Louise laughed. "Forty."

"Give those percentages in public and I'll be destroyed for the rest of my life. My reputation is completely in your hands."

"Trust me."

"I don't see that I have any other option, now that you've learned the secret of the real me."

"The secret of the *real* you?"

He nodded. "Being only forty percent —"

"Jack, you know how good you are," she said, shifting the tone of her voice.

Boxer realized that she'd turned serious, but he still wanted the repartee between them to remain light. "Now don't try to make me feel good. The damage is done. I might never be able to manage another erection, much less an orgasm."

Louise laughed and lay back on the air mattress with her hands behind her head. Her bare breasts were only a shade or two lighter than the rest of her. "The truth is that I am finding it hard to feel guilty about being here," she said.

"You mean you've actually been trying to feel guilty?" Boxer questioned.

She shrugged, and the movement set her breasts in motion for a moment.

"Well, all I can say is that I hope you fail. Feeling guilty about enjoying yourself is about as ridiculous as trying to escape from your problems by drinking."

"Are you sure you're not a shrink?" she asked, squinting up at him.

"Only to my friends."

"So I'm only a friend?"

"A very good one."

"Is that what you tell the other women you sleep with?"

Again the conversation was taking a serious turn that Boxer had no inclination to follow. What he told or didn't tell the other women in his life was his concern alone. He wagged his forefinger at her. "I much prefer to leave that to your imagination. Besides, I was brought up in the tradition that required a man to —"

"Not tell tales out of the school," Louise said, finishing the sentence for him.

"Neither school nor the bedroom," he added.

For a moment, neither of them spoke, then she said, "I have the distinct feel that, as the expression goes, I've just been put in my place."

Boxer smiled. "I'd never do that to a good friend."

"The hell you wouldn't! You'd do that and more, if you thought it would achieve your goal."

"Goal, what goal?"

"To keep you — the real you — in splendid isolation."

"Ah, now you sound like my shrink," Boxer answered.

"Touché!" Louise exclaimed, suddenly rising on her elbows.

Boxer leaned over and gently touched his lips to hers.

"You're an easy man to love," she whispered, "or to be more precise, an easy man to want to love. But very difficult, maybe even impossible, to know."

Boxer kissed her again, then moved his lips to her neck, then to the nipple on her right breast to the one on the left, lingering on each to savor the warmth it had gained from the sun.

Easing herself slowly down on the air mattress again, Louise caressed the back of his head. "You have a way with a woman," she told him.

He smiled down at her. "Maybe it's the other way around. Maybe it's you who have a way with a man."

"Here, on the deck?" she asked in a low throaty voice.

Boxer was about to answer, when suddenly an unfamiliar strumming in the *Sea Dog*'s rigging caused him to look up, and the same time the boat heeled a few degrees more to the port side than before.

He sat up on his haunches, listened a moment longer, then he called out, "Stark, did you hear that?"

"Got two blips at zero-eight-five, at twenty miles —"

"The wind," Boxer called out. He wasn't the slightest bit interested in anything that faraway. "Check the —"

"The barometer is off," Stark answered.

Boxer scrambled to his feet.

"Down two-tenths and dropping," Stark said.

"Looks like we're coming into bad weather," Stark said. "We'll run under power."

Louise sat up, quickly donning her skimpy bikini top.

"Pepe," Boxer called. "Pepe, on deck... We have to take in sail." He ran to the lines controlling the sail on the mainmast.

Louise followed him. "Can I do anything?"

"Hold this line, and when I say 'pay out,' let it go slowly," Boxer said.

Pepe came up through the companionway and immediately ran to the fore lines. Odah was right behind him.

By now the wind was strong enough to sigh in the rigging, and dark gray clouds began to spill over the sky. The sun was gone.

"Pay out!" Boxer shouted.

The mainsail began to come down. The *Sea Dog* was beginning to pitch and roll in response to the sea which was now roiled by the wind.

Boxer pulled, gathering the nylon to the long boom.

"I'm going to turn her into the wind," Stark said, now having to shout above the sound of the wind to make himself heard.

Moments later Boxer heard the dual one hundred horsepower diesels kick in.

"My God, where did those clouds come from?" Louise yelled, shivering from the sudden drop in the ambient temperature.

"Happens like that at sea," Boxer said, lashing the boom securely in its place. "Better get below, and get into something warmer."

"Is that an order?" she questioned, smiling at him.

Boxer shook his head.

"Will you come with me?"

He was about to ask why she wanted him, but she spoke first. "We have something to finish."

Boxer grinned at her. "Yes, we do, don't we?"

"I'm a stickler when it comes to finishing what I start," she said.

"I'll join you as soon as I make sure everything is lashed down that should be lashed down," he answered.

Louise nodded, slipped under the boom, and quickly vanished behind the closed companionway door.

Boxer went aft. Pepe and Odah were already with Stark.

"The bar dropped another tenth," Stark said. "Looks as if we might be in a tropical depression."

"Can we raise any of the weather stations on the radio?"

"Yes, but there's too much static to get a clear message."

"Pepe, try getting a ship to give us a weather report," Boxer said. "Better use the main set." Then he dropped his eyes to the radar screen. There were still two targets on it, approximately twenty miles away, but now at 195 degrees. Because of the heavy sea, they weren't visible all of the time, which meant they couldn't have been much bigger than the *Sea Dog*. He pursed his lips. That they had changed their course to match the *Sea Dog*'s could be just coincidental, or —

Pepe popped his head out of the open companionway door. "We seemed to have met Typhoon Lilly," he shouted. "Picked up a transmission between the *Kobe Maru* and the Hong Kong weather station."

"Stay on the radio," Boxer shouted back, then to Stark, he said, "We had better try for the nearest land. We might have to beach her."

Stark nodded.

"I'll check the charts and give you a new heading in a few minutes," Boxer said.

"I'd like something hot," Stark told him.

"Sure thing," Boxer answered, and quickly made his way below deck, where Louise was waiting for him in his cabin.

"We're going to make a run of the nearest port," he told her. He was glad to be out of the cold driving rain.

"Then this isn't just a squall?" she asked.

"We seem to be on the edge of a typhoon," Boxer answered, taking the opportunity to change his bathing trunks for a waterproof jogging suit. He saw that she too had put on a jogging suit, though hers was a stylish green one, unlike his simple gray.

"Tell Jose that I want hot broth brought topside, enough for myself, Stark, and Paskudnyak. It's going to be a hard few hours before we reach shelter."

"Can I do anything to help?" she asked, following him out of the cabin and into the small below-deck bridge area.

"Not that I can think of now," Boxer answered as he started to study the chart of the ocean area that was spread out on the chart table. "Help Jose in the galley. We'll need sandwiches in a little while."

She went over to him and kissed him on the cheek.

He gave her a quizzical look.

"That's to remind you that I'm still here," she said.

Boxer nodded and resumed studying the chart. He didn't even realize that Louise had left the bridge. Within moments, he'd located Yutz, an island less than ten miles to the southeast.

"Yutz," Boxer shouted into the wind and the rain, as soon as he was on deck again.

Stark was having trouble holding the wheel.

"Yutz," Boxer yelled, now, in front of Stark.

Stark shook his head. "Never heard of it."

"Slightly less than ten miles from here, to the northeast," Boxer told him.

"The wind is coming from the north," Stark told him. "We'll have even more trouble if we swing off to the northeast."

"We can't hold this course or, for that matter, any other course much longer," Boxer said.

At that precise moment, Paskudnyak poked his head up through the open companionway. "We're taking water," he shouted.

"Pumps —"

"Can't handle it."

"Any ships nearby?" Stark shouted.

"Nearest one is four hours away, maybe six," Paskudnyak answered.

"Signal her," Boxer said. "Give her our position. Tell her we're heading for Yutz."

"Yutz?" Paskudnyak questioned.

"Send the fucking message," Boxer yelled, then to Stark he said, "Go below, put on some warm dry clothing, and tell Jose I'm waiting for that hot broth to be brought topside."

Stark hesitated.

"What's wrong?" Boxer asked.

Grinning, Stark said, "I always knew there'd come a time when you'd give the orders."

Boxer grinned too. "So did I," he answered, taking the helm. It took all his strength to begin to bring the *Sea Dog* over to a new heading. She wasn't answering the helm as smartly as she usually did, and as she began to turn, a huge wave lifted her and slammed her down. Water cascaded all over the boat.

Boxer was suddenly afraid she'd founder. She began to climb out of the trough, but was slammed down again by another cascade of water.

Boxer switched on the loudspeaker. "All hands lay topside," he shouted. "All hands, lay topside." He wanted everyone on deck just in case the worst happened.

Paskudnyak was topside first, followed by Odah, then Jose and Louise, and finally Stark. All of them wore their life jackets. They joined him aft.

"If we have to abandon ship, remember to pull the release cord of the automatic distress signaler," Boxer told them.

"No chance of launching the inflatable?" Stark asked.

Boxer shook his head. "Not in this kind of sea," he answered.

Suddenly the *Sea Dog* crested a huge wave, then plunged into another deep trough.

"Here it comes," Boxer shouted, above the roar of the wind. "Hold tight!"

A huge avalanche of boiling white water smashed down on the *Sea Dog*, snapping its mast. It tore Jose loose from the line he held, hurling him into the chaos of white water.

"Take the conn," Boxer shouted to Paskudnyak and, grabbing the Marine-issue K-Bar, he dove into the roiling water. Just before he went, Boxer heard Stark yell, "Shark, closing fast."

He surfaced immediately.

"Shark," Stark shouted, pointing off to the right.

Not more than fifteen feet from himself, Boxer spotted Jose. He was thrashing wildly to keep afloat.

"A line," Boxer yelled.

Almost immediately, Paskudnyak hurled a coil of half-inch nylon line to him. With a lucky grab, Boxer just managed to get hold of it before it vanished into the seething water.

A strong swimmer, Boxer made it to Jose within moments.

"I'm going down," Jose shouted. "I'm going down."

"Get this line around you," Boxer answered.

"Holy mother of God, save me!" Jose yelled.

Boxer looped the line around Jose and, just as he was about to tie it, he glanced to his right. The shark's black fin was clearly visible.

"We don't have much time," Boxer shouted above the sound of the storm. "Secure that line around you, and I'll worry about the shark."

Boxer made a half-turn and saw that the shark had also turned and was beginning to circle.

"Start pulling yourself toward the boat," Boxer ordered.

"Yes, toward the boat," Jose answered, pulling hand over hand on the line, while Boxer swam slowly behind him. He knew the shark would stop circling and start to follow.

They were close enough to the *Sea Dog* for Paskudnyak and Stark to reach down, grab hold of Jose, and pull him aboard.

"Your turn," Stark shouted above the din of the storm.

Boxer let himself be grabbed by Paskudnyak's and Stark's eager hands.

"You're too fucking old to be a shark fighter," Stark said, handing him a cup of hot broth.

"Now you tell me," Boxer answered. "Where were you when I thought I was Captain Ahab and that shark was Moby Dick?"

"That was your last complex," Stark answered. "I thought you were over it."

Boxer looked straight at him. "There are some things a man never gets over, and one of them is my hatred for sharks."

Stark looked at Paskudnyak. "I can't deal with this now. I've got to get us to Yutz, or all of us might be shark bait." Just as he finished speaking, a bolt of lightning struck the mainmast and splintered it. The instantaneous boom of thunder that followed, like a giant hand, closed over the *Sea Dog* and shook it from stem to stern.

"Holy Christ!" Stark exclaimed.

"You can say that again," Boxer said. "We might yet need to say a few holys."

Paskudnyak managed to swallow hard.

The two women came running aft.

"My God, another one like that, and we'll be —"

"A lucky shot," Boxer commented.

"Better cut away all the lines and get that broken mast over the side," Stark said, "or it will begin to throw us around."

Boxer and Paskudnyak cut the lines and together heaved the sheered-off section over the side. Then they returned to the cockpit.

"We'd be able to see Yutz, if it weren't for the rain," Stark said to the two of them.

Boxer checked the radar screen. "It's on the radar, about two miles from where we are."

"Now let's see if we can get inside its cove," Stark said.

"We still have two targets ... at two-seventy," Boxer commented.

"Can you ID the cove?" Stark asked.

Boxer adjusted several dials. "Come to eight-five," he said.

"Steady, as she goes, and we'll make the cove," Boxer said.

The boom of the surf was continuous now.

"If we miss the entrance and get caught up in that surf —" Stark began.

"Ease her over to the port," Boxer said, studying the amber radar display.

Stark turned the helm over.

"Good."

"I see the island!" Louise suddenly shouted. "There, there!" She pointed directly ahead of them. "There!" And she grabbed hold of Boxer's arm. "Do you see it, Jack?"

Boxer looked up. The island was a huge dark, cone-shaped mass.

"Looks like a volcano," Paskudnyak said.

"Probably isn't active," Stark answered. "But even if it were, it's our only hope."

Through the blinding rain, Yutz's shape became more distinct: it was cylindrical and topped by a volcanic cone.

"That cove must be the only safe harbor on the island," Paskudnyak said.

Neither Boxer or Stark answered.

Almost an instant later, they saw the cove dead ahead. It was nothing more than a narrow slit, not more than a hundred yards wide.

Stark pushed the throttle forward.

The *Sea Dog* shuddered, but didn't speed up appreciably.

"We'll make it," Boxer said.

"I was hoping to make it sooner than later," Stark answered.

The wind dropped suddenly, and the water, while still rough, was not anywhere as violent as it had been.

This time when Stark pushed the throttle forward, the *Sea Dog* responded, and, within a matter of minutes, she was between the sheer cliffs of the cove, which turned out to be small, indeed, with little more than a half-mile width, and possessing a narrow, almost semi-circular strip of black volcanic sand for beach.

"We'll be safe enough in here," Stark said, cutting back on the throttle until the *Sea Dog* just had steerage way.

"Come on, let's get the hook over the side," Boxer said to Paskudnyak.

"Aye, aye, sir," he answered.

"Jose," Boxer shouted on the way to the bow, "how about something good to eat?"

"You got it," Jose answered.

Boxer eased the *Sea Dog*'s anchor over the side, and let it drop. When the line stopped running out, he said, "Make it fast."

"Done," Paskudnyak answered.

"Good. Now let's have a drink," Boxer said, feeling much relieved that for the present time they were safe. "I'm for that!" Paskudnyak exclaimed.

CHAPTER 2

Rain still splattered over the *Sea Dog*'s deck, but the wind had died, except for the heaving restlessness of the water that rocked the boat and made it tug at its anchor line.

Below deck, Boxer, Stark, and their guests relaxed in the yacht's main salon, after having eaten a wonderful roast beef that Jose had prepared. Stark occupied the head of the table; Boxer was at the other end; Paskudnyak at Stark's left. The women sat to the right of their male companion.

"I guess now is the time to tell all of you good folks that we're in something of a bind," Stark said.

Boxer had hoped to keep this bad news from his guests until the next morning. Things tended to appear less ominous when the sun was shining than in the dark of night, made darker by heavy cloud cover.

"Bind?" Odah questioned. "What do you mean?"

Boxer replied, "We just might get the chance to play castaways for real."

"How real?" Paskudnyak asked.

"Well, our mainmast is gone, we're low on fuel, and you told me our radio is out."

"You mean, like we're in the twilight zone?"

"That's one way of putting it," Boxer said, smiling. As far as he was concerned, Paskudnyak was, except for those times when he was on the bridge of a submarine, a perpetual resident of the twilight zone. "We'll be out of touch with the rest of the world until we either reach a place where we will be able to radio our whereabouts or repair our own radio."

"What's the next nearest landfall?" Louise asked.

"About a hundred and fifty nautical miles from here," Stark answered. "If we go very slow and we're lucky, we have just enough fuel to make it."

"How slow is slow?" Paskudnyak asked.

"Three knots — max."

"That makes it just about two days' sailing," Boxer commented.

"Three," Stark said. "To be sure that we don't run out of fuel, we better travel at two knots. That's just enough to move the *Sea Dog* along and hold steerage way."

"Maybe we can jury-rig a mast," Paskudnyak offered.

"If we could find a tree on the island that would serve as a mast, we'd be able to. But my guess is that we won't. It's just a volcanic uplift from the ocean, a mountain that's still rising."

"What about food and water?" Odah questioned.

"No problem there. Jose says we have a ten-day supply of food, and with the emergency water tanks, at least double that for water," Stark answered.

"All right, let's get down to the nitty-gritty," Paskudnyak said.

"What's the 'nitty-gritty'? Or, more to the point, what's your 'nitty-gritty'?" Boxer asked.

"Do we have enough booze on board?"

"Enough," Boxer said.

"Absolutely."

Paskudnyak nodded his head vigorously. "I just wanted to be sure that we didn't lack — "

"I heard that too," Boxer said, suddenly standing. Something had bumped against the *Sea Dog*. Just as he was about to move, the companionway door was thrown open.

"Stay where you are!" a man ordered.

Boxer froze.

The next instant the muzzle of a rifle appeared, immediately followed by the man who held it. "You prisoners," he said, now waving the rifle at them.

"Who the hell are you?" Paskudnyak asked, "and where the hell did you get that M-18 from?" The M-18 was the most advanced automatic rifle in the world. Each round it fired was a heat-seeking minimissile.

"Shmuh Geh Gee," the man answered, slapping his chest with his free hand. He was a man of middle size, a Eurasian with a long chintzlike mustache, and black hair set in queue. Two bandoleers of ammunition crisscrossed his chest, a .357 automatic was strapped around his waist, and a sheathed trench knife hung from his belt.

Stark repeated his name.

"You know me?" Shmuh Geh Gee asked, looking curiously at Stark.

"Only by reputation," Stark said.

Shmuh Geh Gee laughed. "Bad, huh?"

"Very bad," Stark answered. "He and his half-brother Fong Shun Un are wanted by practically every government in the world for piracy, murder, rape, and other crimes."

"How do you know about them?" Boxer asked.

"Official reports, and *Play Time* ran an interview of them."

"Who the hell is that bum?" Paskudnyak asked.

"Bum, I not bum. I son of Captain Klaus Mittenkope."

"That name rings a bell," Boxer said.

"Too much talk," Shmuh Geh Gee said. "Everyone topside. Everyone prisoners." Then he shouted something in a combination of Chinese, Malaysian, and what sounded like German to his men on deck. "Okay, topside... You first," he said, pointing the rifle at Boxer, who was already standing.

Boxer hesitated.

"Go!" Shmuh Geh Gee ordered. "Go, or your head blows off."

"You hold all the cards," Boxer answered, and he began to move.

"I no hold cards, I hold rifle," Shmuh Geh Gee growled.

"This isn't what I planned," Boxer said, glancing back at the others around the table.

"Yeah, that's what you're telling us," Paskudnyak answered. "But —"

"No talk!" Shmuh Geh Gee barked.

"I wouldn't push him," Stark whispered.

"Okay, Shmuh Geh Gee, you hold all the cards. No talk," Paskudnyak said.

"Hold fuckin' rifle. No hold cards," Shmuh Geh Gee shouted, going red in the face and waving the rifle in front of him. "No cards... No cards... See? Rifle."

The rain had all but stopped, the wind was down, and there were patches of star-studded sky visible.

On deck there were a dozen other men, all armed the same way as Shmuh Geh Gee. And some of them even looked fiercer.

Shmuh Geh Gee left a prize crew of three men aboard the *Sea Dog*, and transferred Boxer, Stark, and their guests to inflatables, which were then paddled over to two high-speed motor torpedo boats.

"The two targets on the radar," Boxer whispered to Stark.

"No doubt about it. But where the hell did they get them from?"

"Probably from Nam, after we pulled out," Boxer answered.

Within minutes Boxer and the others were aboard one of the boats.

Shmuh Geh Gee ordered them below to the galley, then had one of his men tie their hands behind them.

Paskudnyak was about to complain, when Boxer snapped, "Stow it, sailor." Then he said, "Right now our best bet is to be cool, calm, and collected. To wait to see what happens."

"We start," Shmuh Geh Gee said, and, moving to the boat's bridge, he gave the orders to get under way. Then he returned to the galley, poured himself a generous shot of the scotch from a bottle he had taken from *Sea Dog* and gulped it down. He drank two more before pointing to Louise and Odah. "Bring good money. Maybe ten thousand Hong Kong dollar."

The two women looked dismayed.

"You're going to sell them?" Stark asked.

Paskudnyak, now red in the face, started to stand, but Shmuh Geh Gee pushed him down.

"No stand," the pirate said. "No stand."

"I'll give you twenty thousand American dollars for them," Boxer said calmly.

Shmuh Geh Gee's eyes opened wide. Then he said, "You have no money here."

"No, but I can get it for you," Boxer said.

Shmuh Geh Gee poured himself another drink.

"Women bring good price. Sell to buyer who comes to our village. Maybe go to Bangkok or to the Arabs. Last maybe two, three year then sold again to work for man in the street."

Both women began to silently cry.

Shmuh Geh Gee looked at them with disgust, then he gulped down the drink he'd poured for himself.

"This pleasure cruise is turning out to be a lot less pleasure than I might have had if I had stayed home," Boxer commented under his breath.

"You can say that again," Paskudnyak said.

"No talk," Shmuh Geh Gee growled. "Now talk finish. No say, 'you hold all the cards.'"

"Well, we sure as hell don't," Paskudnyak said.

Shmuh Geh Gee swung his fist over the table and slammed it into Paskudnyak's face. "No talk!" he roared.

Blood poured from Paskudnyak's nose.

"No talk," Shmuh Geh Gee said, his voice much lower. He then stood up and staggered forward to the bridge.

Stark leaned close to Boxer and whispered, "I don't think we have much of a chance of getting out of this alive."

Boxer was thinking much the same thing, but then it occurred to him that Shmuh Geh Gee would have killed him, Stark, and Paskudnyak without batting the proverbial eyelash, unless he had orders to bring all his prisoners back to the village. He said as much to Stark.

"I hope you're right. Maybe there's someone with whom we could bargain," Stark responded.

Suddenly Paskudnyak fell forward, his head crashing on to the table.

"Loss of blood," Boxer said.

Stark nodded.

"Yutz. Who would have thought that we'd be followed here?" Stark said in his characteristically gravelly voice. "After all, Yutz isn't one of those island tourist places. You'd really have to want to go there to even know it existed, unless you were in an extreme situation, such as we were in."

"Such as we *are* in," Boxer responded.

"In that interview I read —"

"I can't believe Shmuh Geh Gee and Fong Shun Un were really the subject for an interview," Boxer said. "For Christ's sake, there must be more important people, let alone, more interesting and successful people to interview."

"Certainly there are, but none of them are pirates; sharks and barracudas, yes, but none of them follow the *Jolly Roger*; and certainly not as willing to speak about their infamous calling, as were Shmuh Geh Gee and Fong Shun Un."

"Thanks for the info, Admiral," Boxer said.

"I still take full responsibility for choosing Yutz," Stark said glumly.

"Yutz is Yutz… It's gone. Now we have to worry about getting all of us out of this mess alive. Besides, I was the one who found it on the map. Remember?"

Stark didn't answer.

"How do you think I feel about this?"

Stark still didn't answer.

"Since you're so interested, I'll tell you. I feel — well, I feel like an idiot. No, I feel rotten."

"I'm glad," Stark said.

"Glad that I feel rotten?"

"Proves you're getting better, Jack. I wasn't sure. Yes, yes, I know you relate well to Louise, but you know, unlike yourself, I never believed that your excess sexual energy was an indication of anything more than a combination of active gonads and a similarly active imagination."

"You're joking."

"Have I ever joked with you?"

For several moments, Boxer thought, then he said, "Not that I can remember."

"I mean, Jack, all your humping only means —"

"Tell me later... We're slowing down," Boxer said.

"I might not have the chance," Stark responded.

Boxer nodded. "All right, tell me now."

"Very adolescent."

"You're joking — sorry, I know you never joke."

"Hasn't it ever struck you that way?"

"I can't say that it has. But what does strike me is that this is a very weird conversation to be having now. If this has been your feeling —"

"It has."

"Then you should have brought the subject up before this. Given that Mittenkope is as crazy as Shmuh Geh Gee, I might not ever hump again. Dead men never hump, at least as far as I know."

"What bothers you more: the possibility that you might be dead, or that you might not be able to hump again?"

"I'm not exactly thrilled by either prospect," Boxer answered. "But since you asked a very profound question, Admiral, I'll answer it. Being dead, at least as far as I know, is being nowhere, while humping, however adolescent the pursuit might be, gives both participants a wonderful sense of gratification when the actual humping is completed."

Paskudnyak suddenly raised his head, looked at the two of them, and said, "And I thought I was dreaming this whole thing."

"Don't think you're the only one," Louise said. "Odah and I are awake, and we feel that not only are we in the middle of someone else's nightmare, but somehow we're also entangled in some wild male philosophical musings about humping, which defies definition, philosophical or otherwise."

Shmuh Geh Gee came down the companionway. "Soon we tie up, and you see Captain Mittenkope," he announced.

"Your dear ol' dad," Stark said.

Shmuh Geh Gee glowered at him.

"Sorry. I didn't know that things were that way between the two of you."

Shmuh Geh Gee pointed the M-18 at him. "I put hole in your head, then you shut mouth."

Boxer said, "He's an old man, and old men talk too much. You know that."

Shmuh Geh Gee turned his attention and the M-18 to Boxer. Boxer forced himself to laugh.

"What funny?" Shmuh Geh Gee asked, his eyes narrowing.

"My friend doesn't think bang-bang good for you," Boxer said, using the island slang to get across his point.

Shmuh Geh Gee's eyes widened a bit. He glanced at Stark, then at the two women. "Old man no bang-bang?" he asked.

Boxer shook his head.

"For Christ's sake, this is going too far," Stark muttered under his breath.

"He doesn't know it, but we're playing poker. And I'm holding all the cards."

"Look again," Stark said. "He's the guy holding the M-18."

Boxer smiled. "I'm still ahead. I see what he has, but he can't see what I have."

"What you talkin' about?" Shmuh Geh Gee asked.

"About bang-bang."

"What about bang-bang?"

"He says he still can bang-bang," Boxer answered.

Shmuh Geh Gee grinned and nodded vigorously. "Man who can't bang-bang better off dead."

Suddenly one of Shmuh Geh Gee's men poked his head into the salon and spoke in the strange patois they had heard before.

"Meet Mittenkope now," Shmuh Geh Gee said, waving the M-18 toward the companionway stairs. "On feet, everybody."

"I guess this is what you might call a command performance," Boxer said as he stood.

CHAPTER 3

When Boxer and the others left Shmuh Geh Gee's mob, the storm had all but vanished, leaving only its memory in windblown clouds already coloring pink with the first light in the east. The quay on which they stood was made of wood, and at the end of it was a short, reedlike old man whose grizzled face sported a black patch over his left eye. He wore a pair of spotless white pants and the white officer's cap of the Nazi *Kriegsmarine*.

"Mittenkope," Boxer stage-whispered to the others.

"It couldn't be Admiral Raider," Stark growled.

"Wasn't he hanged?" Paskudnyak asked.

"No talkie," Shmuh Geh Gee ordered.

"No talkie," Boxer echoed.

"He doesn't look very piratical to me," Louise commented.

"We're probably seeing his better side," Boxer said.

"I'd make him to be my age," Stark commented.

"Hardly as old as that," Boxer snapped.

"No talkie!" Shmuh Geh Gee shouted.

"That man has a one-track mind," Odah whispered.

Boxer and his party walked another two yards, then they were halted, and Shmuh Geh Gee called out, "Bring prisoners." And immediately switching into that strange mixture of German and local island dialect, he began a long-winded explanation, complete with vigorous gesticulations.

Mittenkope gave no indication that he was listening, but when Shmuh Geh Gee finally stopped, he said in perfect English, "I am honored to have such renowned guests."

Stark spoke. "We're not your guests, Captain. According to Shmuh Geh Gee, we're your prisoners."

Mittenkope shook his head. His right hand making a slight back and forth motion, he said, "This pirate business, I'm afraid, has gone to his head. Next thing you know, he'll be wearing a black patch over one eye."

"I wonder where he'd get that idea from," Paskudnyak commented.

"Not that we'd want to be ungrateful, but none of us have the time to be your guests," Boxer said. "All of us have other things to do."

Mittenkope nodded, then he said, "And so have I, Admiral Boxer, so have I."

"Obviously Shmuh Geh Gee went through the *Sea Dog*'s papers," Boxer responded, and, turning to the women, he introduced them first, then Stark, Paskudnyak, and finally Jose.

Mittenkope clicked his heels together for the ladies, saluted Stark and Paskudnyak, and nodded to Jose. Looking over his right shoulder toward the sun which was already above the horizon, he said, "Now we have breakfast." He barked out an order, turned, and led the way up a wide dirt path that began where the quay ended.

Still under guard, Boxer and his companions followed Captain Mittenkope up a wide path that led to the top of a hill where there was a lovely house built of coconut logs, island stone, and stout timbers that had obviously come from wrecked ships. It looked very much like an illustration out of a boy's adventure book. But it was real, complete with the booty taken from dozens of bloody pirate forays against hapless ships.

"Welcome to my home," Mittenkope said, bowing slightly from the waist, as though he were greeting guests, not prisoners. "The best thing about it is the view from either porch, front or rear. From the one in the front, I can watch the sun come up, and from the one in the rear, I can see it set."

Before Boxer or anyone else could speak, Mittenkope barked another order in the patois and then announced that dinner would be served in ten minutes. "While we wait," he said, "I suggest that you take the opportunity to wash up. Please consider my humble home your vacation villa."

"It's kind of hard to have the necessary good feelings, Captain, with armed guards —"

Mittenkope raised his right hand. "Say no more. Shmuh Geh Gee frequently does things that are — how would you say — ?"

"Stupid," Paskudnyak responded.

"To put it a bit more delicately — less than wise," Mittenkope said. Then, speaking in English, he told his son that the armed guards were not needed. "I consider these people my guests."

"May be your guest, but my prisoner," Shmuh Geh Gee answered surlily. "I capture."

"Nothing is more bitter to a father than a weird son," Stark commented.

"Or daughter," added Louise.

"Women go with me," Shmuh Geh Gee said.

"No way!" Boxer said, stepping forward.

Shmuh Geh Gee whirled and pointed his M-18 at Boxer. "You dead man!"

"No, you're dead," Mittenkope snapped. He was holding a .22 automatic in his right hand, and the muzzle was pointed straight at Shmuh Geh Gee's head.

"Wow, this is some tableau," Paskudnyak whispered, "and before breakfast too. Imagine what we'll have to entertain us later."

Shmuh Geh Gee's brow knitted. He then took a deep breath, and after slowly exhaling, said, "Not worth fighting over. Women not cherry!"

Mittenkope smiled and said, "He's a good boy at heart."

"You could have fooled me," Stark whispered to Boxer.

"Me too. But a father has to take a positive attitude, even though the child is very negative."

"Well, people, take whatever time you need to freshen up," Mittenkope said, then, making the correct assumption about who was sleeping with whom, he assigned rooms to his guests. "All of your personal belongings have been brought ashore and placed in your respective rooms," he told them.

Boxer thanked him, and, placing his arm around Louise's waist, he quickly guided her to their room. He not only had an intense desire to hold her in his arms, but he also wanted time to think about what had happened to him and his friends, and what was yet to come…

"I can't believe this," Louise said in a small voice. "Is Mittenkope for real, and that Shmuh Geh Gee — "

"They're both for real," Boxer answered.

"How are we going to get out of this?" she asked.

Boxer walked the length of the room, which was at least twenty feet across and just as wide, furnished with an assortment of styles that ranged from American Colonial to Swedish Modern. Everything, no doubt, had been taken from captured vessels.

"You haven't answered my question," Louise pressed. "This island may be named Yutz, but I'm beginning to think Loony Island would have been a more apt name."

Boxer went to the window which looked out on the wide porch beyond, to the steep slope that led to a surf-pounded beach. "It would be suicide to try to launch a boat in that surf."

Louise had come up beside him. "Looks that way, doesn't it?"

Boxer put his arm around her shoulders and squeezed. "As the saying goes, we'll just have to play it by ear. We don't have any choice."

"What do you think will happen to us?" she asked.

"That's what we will find out, I hope, at dinner," he answered.

She pressed herself close to him. "Do you think we'll get out of this — I mean, all of us?" she whispered.

Boxer shrugged. He wasn't going to give her any false hopes, but neither did he want to increase her fear. "I don't really know. So far, other than being held against our will, nothing has been done to us."

"Maybe someone will come looking for us?" she offered, moving away from him.

"Maybe," Boxer answered, though he knew that wouldn't start — if it would start at all — until at least seventy-two hours had passed, after they were due to arrive in Singapore and that was still two days away.

It took them a few minutes to dress, and when they rejoined Mittenkope in the living room, Stark was already there, apparently enjoying a lively conversation with the old Nazi.

The dinner was sumptuous, with a variety of savory meat and seafood dishes, tropical vegetables, and wines, which

Mittenkope proudly boasted came from the various ships his sons and their men had attacked.

Naturally, Mittenkope sat at the head of the table; Stark was opposite him.

The four waiters who served the food were dressed in a variety of clothes, wore white gloves, and performed their work with totally expressionless faces.

When coffee was served, and cigars handed to the men, Mittenkope said, as he lit his cigar, "I was responsible for sinking the British cruiser *Edinburgh* —"

"Ah, that's why the name rang a bell!" Boxer exclaimed. "You're Klaus Mittenkope."

"Then you've heard about me," Mittenkope said, smiling broadly.

"Wasn't the *Edinburgh* carrying a fortune in gold?" Boxer asked.

"Estimates vary, but the figure most accepted is four hundred million, and that was at the American price then of thirty-five dollars an ounce."

Paskudnyak gave a low whistle. "Now at four hundred dollars an ounce — my God, that has to be several billion."

Mittenkope blew a cloud of bluish white smoke toward the ceiling. "She's down in eight hundred feet of water," he said.

Stark entered the conversation. "Is *der Kapitän* trying to tell us that he knows where the *Edinburgh* is?"

"I have the exact position marked on my chart," he answered, chuckling.

Pointing his cigar at Mittenkope, Boxer said, "And you want us to help you get the gold, right?"

"Only part right," Mittenkope answered. "I want to go home to the Fatherland, to Germany, before I die. I want you to take me. In exchange, I will help you get the gold."

"Wait, a damn minute!" Paskudnyak exclaimed. "Why can't you just go and —"

"My sons," Mittenkope answered, cutting Paskudnyak short. Then in a choked voice and with tears leaking out of the corner of his aged eye, he said, "I am a prisoner here, just as much as all of you are. They are afraid I will help the authorities capture them." He paused and used the white linen table napkin to wipe his eyes.

"They got that idea from their mother, Zoineh. She's Chinese and Arab. It's hard for me to tell you this, but my sons don't have any of my genes. There's nothing German about them. Nothing!" he exclaimed, then using the linen table napkin, he not only wiped his eyes with it, but loudly blew his nose into it.

Boxer looked at Stark, who in turn looked at Paskudnyak, who was making sympathetic clicking sounds with his tongue. Then, in a voice filled with commiseration, he said, "My father — may he rest in peace — was a man of a very few words, but he always said, 'A man whose sons are worthless, disrespectful, or just plain nasty has a very heavy load to carry.'"

Boxer looked quizzically at his friend.

"That's what my old man always said," Paskudnyak told him.

Stark asked, "If you can't get off this island, how can we?"

Mittenkope put his cigar down in an ashtray made from a coconut shell, leaned forward, and, planting his elbows on the table, he whispered, "Before I tell you that, I have to have your assurances that you will help me return to Germany."

"That's reasonable," Stark said and looked at Boxer, who nodded.

"I'll go with that," Paskudnyak said.

"You certainly have my assurance," Louise told him.

"And mine, likewise," Odah added.

Mittenkope nodded. Still speaking in a whisper, he said, "By submarine, by my boat, the Sixty-nine" An instant later he guffawed. "Yes, yes, it's here. It's always been here... That's how I arrived."

"You want us to believe that the Nazi submarine —"

Mittenkope's right hand suddenly went up. "Wait!" he exclaimed. "Before we go on I want everyone here to understand that I was not a Nazi... I was just doing my job."

"Let's not get into that," Boxer said.

"I insist that you understand that I was a U-boat commander, nothing else."

Boxer nodded. "Okay, I accept it, and I'm sure that all of my colleagues do."

Mittenkope nodded. "I don't want any of you to have a mistaken idea about me," he said.

There was an awkward moment of silence, during which Boxer had some difficulty stopping a smile. The man was a self-acknowledged pirate, and now he wanted them to believe that he hadn't been a card-carrying Nazi!

"Either you tell us what the situation is, or we make our own situation."

Mittenkope glared at him. "Are you threatening me?" he asked in a low menacing voice.

Boxer ignored the question and said, "You already admitted that you're as much a prisoner as we are."

Stark entered the conversation. "The only chance you have of getting off this island and back to Germany, Captain, is to help us get off the island, and you have our word that we'll take you back to the Fatherland."

For several moments, Mittenkope considered what Stark said. Then, he nodded. "All right, I'll tell you. The Sixty-nine is here."

"The submarine?" Boxer asked.

Mittenkope nodded. "Before Germany surrendered, I was ordered to go to Japan and give them the boat. On the way there we were spotted by Japanese destroyers. They mistook the Sixty-Nine for an American submarine and began to attack. I sank two, but the third damaged my boat. But I managed to slip away and came to this island. The rest is history."

"What history?" Stark asked.

Mittenkope, obviously feeling more comfortable, blew several smoke rings before he said, "Neither I nor my men wanted to go back to a defeated Germany. There were people here who welcomed us. We decided to stay. But now I'm the only one left, and it is time to go back."

Stark nodded.

"I have a deep yearning to see the family I left behind," Mittenkope said wistfully.

"You mean you have a wife — " Louise began.

"And a son and daughter. The son bears my name, Klaus, and the daughter is named Gretchen."

"So much for his wild oats," Paskudnyak said. "Let's not get all choked up by this one-eyed pirate's sad tale of woe. Let's get down to the nitty-gritty."

"What's this 'nitty-gritty'?" Mittenkope asked.

"The split, once we get the gold."

"I want a hundred million, at today's market price, for the gold," Mittenkope said, then blew another smoke ring.

"Twenty-five," Paskudnyak snapped.

"Forty."

"Thirty, and that's the bottom line."

"Thirty, done!" Mittenkope exclaimed, spitting on the palm of his hand, then extending it toward Paskudnyak.

"I want to see the boat," Boxer said.

"I assure you that she's completely seaworthy," Mittenkope said. "And I made some design changes that will allow us to operate it with the number of men at the table."

"What about the women?" Odah asked.

"They're coming with us," Boxer said, "or the deal is off."

"It never entered my mind that they wouldn't be coming with us," Mittenkope responded with a leer.

"And Jose the cook," Stark said.

Mittenkope nodded. "Of course."

"When do we leave?" Stark asked.

"The day after tomorrow at oh-four-hundred. The tide will be high enough to float the U-Sixty-nine over the sandbar, and then it's out to sea."

"Fuel?"

"Her tanks have been full for several years."

"Batteries?" Boxer asked. It had been years since he operated a battery-driven boat.

"Fully charged."

"Weapons?" Paskudnyak asked. "I wouldn't want to be caught by your charming sons with nothing to defend us."

"Forward four incher and two machine guns that can be mounted on the conning tower bridge. A hundred rounds for the deck gun. Five thousand round for the machine guns, and four torpedoes that are still operational," Mittenkope finished proudly.

"Are you thinking what I'm thinking?" Boxer asked, looking at Paskudnyak.

"Yeah, leave it to the Germans."

"No."

"No?" Paskudnyak asked with a boyishly innocent expression on his face.

"The four incher and machine guns —"

"Jack, once we're out of here, we dive, and —"

"We won't be able to dive," Mittenkope said. "Run awash, yes, but dive, definitely not. We dive, and we keep going down. We stay down."

Boxer looked at his companions' faces.

"I should have known something was wrong with the plan. It was beginning to sound too easy," Paskudnyak said.

"Nothing is wrong with the plan," Mittenkope responded. "On the surface, the U-Sixty-nine can do twenty-five knots, twenty-eight if she's pushed. Underwater, her top speed is six knots."

"It's the reverse of what our nuclear submarines can do today," Stark explained. "We're faster underwater and slower on the surface."

"My sons and their men will come after us," Mittenkope said. "But the four incher and the machine guns should stop them."

"*Should* is a conditional word," Paskudnyak said. "I'd feel more comfortable with something like *definitely*. It's more comfortable."

"Stay here, and I assure you your women will be taken and sold into prostitution by my sons, and as for yourselves — well, they would find a way to eventually kill you, even though you'd be living here under my protection."

"Just for the record, Captain, the men would be under your protection, but the women wouldn't?" Boxer questioned.

"Pirate rules," Mittenkope said. "Beautiful women, even though — with all due respect — they are not virgins, can be sold for as much as a hundred thousand dollars. That money is always divided among the men."

"Given that situation, I don't see that we have much choice," Stark said.

"None, I'd say," Boxer added.

"None," Paskudnyak said, as he looked lovingly at Odah.

"Good, very good," Mittenkope said, rubbing his hands. "Very good. I can almost smell my wife's roast goose — strange, how you can miss something for so many years…"

"The wife or the goose?" Paskudnyak asked.

The question brought Mittenkope up sharply. He glared at Paskudnyak.

"What the hell, I was just asking," Paskudnyak explained.

Suddenly, Mittenkope started to laugh. "The goose," he said. "The goose… No one here knows how to make roast goose the way Marta did."

"Well, I'll say this for him," Paskudnyak whispered to Boxer, "at least he's honest about that. But — to use an old saw — I wouldn't trust *der Kapitän* as far as I could throw him."

"I don't," Boxer answered. "But he's the only game in town, at least as far as getting off this island goes."

Paskudnyak gave a reluctant nod.

CHAPTER 4

By the time Boxer and his companions finished breakfast, half the morning had gone by, and the cool breeze coming off the ocean had been replaced by steamy atmosphere of that latitude.

"I would like to see the chart that shows the exact location of the *Edinburgh*," Boxer said to Mittenkope, the two of them leaving the dining room together.

"It's aboard the boat. You will see it when we go aboard."

Boxer suddenly had the unpleasant feeling that he was being asked by *der Kapitän* to buy a pig in a poke.

Then, as if Mittenkope could read his thoughts, the former U-boat captain said, "I assure you that I have the charts. But it would arouse suspicion if we should pay a visit to the U-Sixty-nine before our departure. My sons have spies everywhere."

Boxer silently accepted the explanation.

"You and your friends are free to roam the island," Mittenkope told him, "but don't be surprised if you find yourselves being shadowed."

"I'd like to go aboard the *Sea Dog*," Boxer said. "There are some things —"

Mittenkope shook his head. "That would be impossible. Your boat is already on its way to being sold. That's the way it's done when we take a prize. It is sold as quickly as possible. The new owner modifies it, making it almost unrecognizable."

"Neat!" Boxer commented. "A few changes and the *Sea Dog* doesn't exist anymore."

Mittenkope raised his eyebrows. "Neat?" he questioned.

"Just an American expression," Boxer explained. "It means that something is well done, good; that it couldn't be done better."

"Neat," Mittenkope said with a lopsided smile, then he stopped. "Please excuse me, I have some work to attend to." He came to attention, clicked his heels together, and nodded to everyone. "I will see all of you for cocktails at four." He executed a sharp about-face, and strode off.

"All that was missing from that performance was a snappy arm salute," Paskudnyak said sourly.

"Maybe," Stark commented. "But he's our only hope."

"You don't have to cozy up to him," Boxer said, "just don't antagonize him."

"I know… I know," Paskudnyak answered, still looking sour.

"Well, do we tour the island?" Odah asked.

"Might as well," Boxer answered. "I'd like to get a look at the captain's U-Sixty-nine."

"I wonder if that number has some hidden meaning?" Louise questioned with an impish look on her face.

"Only if it's in the dark," Boxer answered.

Louise stuck out her tongue.

"Now, that doesn't have much of a hidden meaning, but it certainly is an open invitation."

"Admiral, you have a unidirectional mind."

Boxer laughed. "The Navy can do that to you."

"Don't blame the Navy," Stark said. "Blame the man."

Boxer started to walk toward the door. "Okay, blame the man. He can take it."

"And he will, every chance he gets," Paskudnyak said as they trooped down the steps.

"Which way?" Odah asked.

"You choose it," Paskudnyak answered.

Odah hesitated for a few moments, then turning to her left, she said, "This way."

"East," Paskudnyak said.

"Smarty pants!" she exclaimed scornfully.

The island proved to be two islands, both circular, and connected by a narrow causeway that had been built on a sandbar. Mittenkope and his band of cutthroats lived on the larger island, which couldn't have been more than a mile wide. Boxer estimated that the smaller island was less than half that. But there was absolutely no sign of the U-69.

Stark, who'd become an amateur naturalist during his retirement, commented, "There's more than enough native fruits and other edible plants to feed Mittenkope's people, and, given these waters, there's an abundance of fish."

"I can't say that I'm concerned about whether or not they are well fed, or even if they eat," Paskudnyak responded. "And I can't say that I'm enjoying this tramp around Captain Mittenkope's fiefdom."

"Are you going to be a spoilsport while the rest of us are having the time of our lives?" Boxer asked as they headed into what was obviously the island village.

"Jack, don't ever again tell me that I'm weird, because you're the weirdest man I know, bar none."

Boxer nodded. "You might be right... You just might be right!"

"Might be," Paskudnyak yelled. "Might be! Louise, you sleep with that man, is he weird or isn't he?"

"Well, now and then he gets a little kinky," she answered with a straight face.

"See, in or out of bed, he's weird," Paskudnyak said triumphantly.

Boxer stopped abruptly. "Hey, what is this — gang up on poor old Jack Boxer?"

The others stopped too, and Paskudnyak said, "Look at these people."

"I'm looking," Boxer said, actually looking at a man and a woman who were staring at them from the open doorway of a small thatched-roof house.

"To borrow a phrase, 'they have a lean and hungry look,'" he said.

"Have you noticed that several of them have one blue eye and one black eye?" Boxer queried.

"No. But what I have noticed is that none of them have smiled at us, not even one of their kids."

"Did you smile at any of them — adults or kids?"

"Okay, Admiral Boxer, see? I'm smiling at those two there in the doorway," Paskudnyak said, forcing a grin on his face. "I don't see them smiling back."

"Maybe they can sense that your heart isn't in it," Boxer offered.

Suddenly the man pulled the woman back and slammed the door shut.

"So much for the smiling technique!" Paskudnyak said. "Have anything else you want to try?"

Boxer shook his head and started to walk again. "One thing is for sure —"

"And what might that be?"

"We're certainly not going to be around long enough to try diplomacy" Boxer said.

"I think we should try to get out of here now," Paskudnyak responded. "I think Mittenkope is off his rocker, or at least half off of it. I think we should take one of the FMTBs, and —"

"We'd be shark bait before we ever cleared the cove," Boxer said, his tone suddenly becoming hard. "We're not playing with just your ordinary brand of gangster. Mittenkope's sons and their men make the Mafia look like boy scouts."

"Okay, if you can tell me where Mittenkope's boat is, then maybe I'll change my mind about him."

Boxer shrugged, but said nothing. He too was beginning to think that Mittenkope's imagination might have been working overtime, or that he might be suffering from some brain disorder; he was at least eighty years old, give or take a year or two.

"Why don't you give the captain a chance to produce," Stark counseled. "After all, if it wasn't for his protection, the two ladies would have been sold off to some brothel keeper, and we three would have been killed."

Paskudnyak considered that for a few moments, then he nodded and said, "You have a point there, Admiral."

"I have the only point," Stark answered.

"But where's the boat?" Paskudnyak asked.

Stark shook his head. "The captain is the only one who can answer that. And we don't have any choice but to wait until he does."

And Boxer added, "That means waiting without antagonizing *der Kapitän*."

"*Moi?* I'm the least antagonistic man here," Paskudnyak answered. "Go on, Odah, tell these worthy officers of the United States Navy how unantagonistic I am.

"He's absolutely unantagonistic ... as long as he gets his way," Odah said with an expressionless face.

Paskudnyak uttered a wordless sound of disgust. "The trouble with you people is that you don't understand the value of questions or dissent."

"You're right," Stark said and quickly added, "Please don't go into an explanation of it now. Save it until we're sitting at a cocktail table in Singapore or some other agreeable place."

"Aye, aye, sir," Paskudnyak answered, highballing Stark, who returned the courtesy.

The man standing in front of Shmuh Geh Gee's desk (the pirate was a man who appreciated a good desk. In that particular room he had seven of them, one for each day of the week) had served breakfast to his father's guests earlier that day.

"You're sure you tell everything, Nudnik?" Shmuh Geh Gee asked in the island dialect.

"Sure."

"Captain plans getaway," Nudnik said. "Go to get gold, much gold with guests."

"Not guests — prisoners. *My* prisoners," Shmuh Geh Gee shouted, banging the top of the desk with his fist. "My prisoners."

Nudnik fell back three steps.

"This time I kill him," Shmuh Geh Gee shouted. "I kill him, take his boat, and I become the captain, and Fong Shun Un must do what *I* say."

Nudnik nodded. He was a short man with a strong desire to be more than just a waiter in the *der Kapitän*'s house, and an even greater desire to have a beautiful woman of his own.

Shmuh Geh Gee's rage vanished just as quickly as it came, and he began to rub his chin. He knew that if he acted without cutting his brother in, he'd have a bigger problem with Fong Shun Un than he might be able to handle.

"You have a plan?" Nudnik asked.

Shmuh Geh Gee blinked and suddenly realized he'd revealed more to Nudnik than he'd wanted to. "Sure, I have plan. You go back to *der Kapitän*'s house."

Nudnik bobbed his head up and down, but didn't move.

"Why aren't you —"

"I want one of the women," Nudnik blurted out.

Shmuh Geh Gee's brow furrowed, then he pointed his finger at him. "You want one of the women?" he questioned.

Nudnik said, "Don't care which."

Shmuh Geh Gee rubbed his chin. "No problem."

Nudnik smiled.

Shmuh Geh Gee smiled.

"Now, I go," Nudnik said, turning around.

Shmuh Geh Gee eased the 9mm automatic out of his belt and, still smiling, he called, "Nudnik?"

The man turned, saw the gun.

Two rapid shots instantly melded into one, and the top of Nudnick's head splattered against the far wall.

"Did you hear that?" Boxer asked, looking at Louise, who was at the window across the room, while he was stretched out on the bed. They'd returned from their walk an hour before, and he'd tried unsuccessfully to nap. He was sitting up now.

"Yes. It's not thunder. There's not a cloud in the sky."

Boxer shook his head. "Shots," he said. "Probably two." He was on his feet, then went to the window and listened. "Not too far from here, from the sound of them!"

There was a knock on the door.

"Paskudnyak," a low voice announced from the other side.

Boxer went to the door and opened it.

"You heard those shots?" Paskudnyak asked.

"Yes."

Suddenly Mittenkope appeared seemingly out of nowhere in the hallway. "There's been a shooting," he said. "Shmuh Geh Gee shot one of the men."

"Does he do that often?" Boxer asked.

"Only when he thinks —"

"That's stretching it," Paskudnyak said.

"It was one of the housemen, a waiter," Mittenkope said.

"Oh, I'm sorry," Louise said. She'd come to the doorway, as had Odah, on the opposite side of the hallway.

"No need to be," Mittenkope said. "I probably would have done the same thing. The man was a spy."

Boxer raised his eyebrows.

Mittenkope nodded. "He was spying for Shmuh Geh Gee."

"How do you know that?"

Mittenkope grinned. "I have my ways of knowing." Then, he added, "Shmuh Geh Gee's room of desks is wired … so is his bedroom."

"Some father-son relationship!" Paskudnyak commented.

Mittenkope looked puzzled.

Boxer hastened to explain. "What he means is that some fathers have very different relationships with their sons than he had with his father."

"Someday you'll have to tell me about it," Mittenkope said, looking at Paskudnyak. Then, turning his attention back to Boxer, he told him, "We'll leave tonight, just before midnight."

"What about the sandbar?" Boxer questioned.

"We'll blow it. Two, maybe three underwater satchel charges should do it."

"I'm ready," Boxer said, looking at his companions.

"I sure as hell am," Paskudnyak answered.

"Me too," Stark added.

"The quicker we get out of here," Louise said, "the happier I'm going to be."

"We must continue to act normally," Mittenkope told them. "I'll gather all of you together when the time comes." He paused, taking a deep breath before he said, "My guess is that Fong Shun Un will be here soon. Shmuh Geh Gee is more brawn than brain. If he thinks something important is going to take place, he'll certainly call his brother, if for no other reason than he would not want to face an angry Fong Shun Un."

"What about you, Captain, do you have any qualms about facing an angry Fong Shun Un?" Stark questioned.

Mittenkope slowly shook his head. "At my age what could happen to me that will not happen soon?" Then he smiled. "That, perhaps, is the only advantage age has over youth."

Stark gave a silent nod of agreement.

The seating arrangement for dinner was slightly different than it had been for lunch. Paskudnyak's and Boxer's position at the table was changed: Paskudnyak now was on Mittenkope's right, and Boxer on his left. Louise now sat next to Paskudnyak, and Odah was alongside Boxer.

As soon as everyone was seated, Mittenkope announced, "Broiled grouper in coconut leaves with wild onion sauce is the main course."

"I'm allergic to anything with onions," Louise said.

Mittenkope gave her a quizzical look.

"I get sick," she explained, and at that precise moment, Shmuh Geh Gee entered the room accompanied by another man, who was a good head and a half taller.

Mittenkope stood up, trembling with rage. He shot something at them in the island dialect. The unknown man replied.

"The prodigal son, no doubt," Stark commented in a stage whisper.

"Yeah, I can see the resemblance," Paskudnyak said. "The three of them look as if they escaped from a Saturday night horror show. Only this one is bigger than either his father or brother, twice as ugly, and twice as mean looking."

"You're interrupting dinner," Mittenkope told his sons, his voice tight with anger.

Fong Shun Un's light blue, hard-looking eyes moved from person to person at the table. Pointing to his father, he said, "I take women an' sell tomorrow."

Paskudnyak started to move.

"They have the odds," Boxer snapped, motioning him to stay where he was.

Glaring at Boxer, Fong Shun Un shouted, "What you say?"

"I said that you were ugly," Boxer answered, taking hold of the bottom of the tablecloth.

"You say —"

"You're ugly."

Fong Shun Un strode up to him.

"Get the other one!" Boxer shouted as he whipped the tablecloth off the table, sending dozens of dishes and pieces of cutlery clattering to the floor. But he got the tablecloth over Fong Shun Un's head before the pirate could move.

Fong Shun Un wildly flailed his arms while Boxer twisted the bottom of the cloth tighter and tighter. "Give me something to tie it off with," he yelled.

"My blouse!" Louise answered.

Boxer held fast to Fong Shun Un, who was half-covered by a sheet.

"Here," Louise said, handing Boxer her blouse.

"Twist it," he said, looking at her. He glanced over at Paskudnyak and Shmuh Geh Gee.

The two of them were rolling on the floor.

Louise handed her blouse back to Boxer.

"This will hold you for a bit," he said, using the blouse to secure the tablecloth around Fong Shun Un.

Suddenly, a loud crack sounded in the room, and Paskudnyak exclaimed, "This one is out!"

Boxer put his hand on Fong Shun Un's shoulder. "Sit," he commanded.

"No sit!"

"You sit, pirate boy," Boxer said, kneeing Fong Shun Un in the groin.

The man went down.

Looking at Paskudnyak, Boxer said, "Disarm that sucker, and tie him up too,"

"That was exceptionally well done," Stark commented.

"With all due respect, sir," Paskudnyak answered, still breathing hard, "you might have helped."

"I did," Stark said. Then, with a wry smile, he added, "I did by staying out of it. The captain and I are too old to —"

"To engage in such violent physical activity," Mittenkope interrupted, finishing the sentence for Stark.

"That's right," Stark said, then he asked, "Where did you learn to do that, Jack?"

"Not at the Academy, that's for sure," Paskudnyak answered.

"In a barroom brawl, a long time ago," Boxer answered.

"It was a lesson well learned," Mittenkope commented.

"To hell with all this chitchat about well-learned lessons!" Louise exclaimed. "I want to know what's going to happen when the two of them are let go?"

"They'll kill you," Mittenkope said.

"First torture, then kill," Fong Shun Un shouted, his voice somewhat muffled by the tablecloth.

Mittenkope gestured to Boxer to follow him.

"Get another shirt," Boxer said to Louise as he left.

"Yes, sir," she snapped, saluting him.

Boxer grinned, then he and Mittenkope were out of the dining room.

"We will leave tonight," Mittenkope said, stopping just on the other side of the doorway, out of the sight and hearing of anyone in the dining room.

"I didn't catch any sign of the U-Sixty-nine," Boxer said.

Mittenkope smiled. "I never said that you would. But I assure you she's real, if that's what you and your companions are worried about."

"What about your sons?"

"I will give each of them an injection with a powerful sedative. They will sleep for at least twelve hours."

Boxer nodded.

"Now, let us return and finish our dinner," Mittenkope said.

Boxer nodded. "I suddenly feel very hungry."

"That was the way I felt after every attack I made," Mittenkope said wistfully. "And, oddly enough, a successful attack always made me feel even more hungry."

"I'm ready for dinner," Boxer announced, re-entering the dining room.

"So am I," Mittenkope said, following close behind him.

Side by side, Boxer and Louise stood close to the open window and looked out at the ocean, now silvered by the light from a thin crescent moon.

"Do you think we'll make it out of here?" Louise asked in a low voice.

Without hesitation, Boxer answered, "Out of here, yes. But Mittenkope's two bandits will come after us."

She faced him. "And you think —"

"They have those MTBs. They're fast, well armed."

Louise smiled wanly. "I guess we'll need some luck," she said,

"Lots of it," Boxer answered, putting his arms around her.

She rested her head on his chest. "This is the first time in my life that I'm in real danger."

Boxer stroked her silky black hair. There wasn't any point in explaining that danger was as much a part of his life as the air they breathed.

"Are you afraid?" Louise asked.

"Yes," he said. "Only a fool isn't afraid when his life is being threatened."

"Hold me tight, Jack!" she said, then offered him her lips.

He kissed her gently.

"I know this is strange, but I need to feel totally alive," she whispered. "I need to be loved, even if it's make-believe."

Boxer kissed her again, and, sweeping her into his arms, he carried her to the bed.

CHAPTER 5

It was three o'clock in the morning when Mittenkope assembled Boxer and his companions in the main sitting room and began handing out M-18s and two bandoleers of ammo to everyone.

"I want to be ready for anything," Mittenkope said as he opened up a box of phosphorous grenades, giving the first three to Stark.

"How about a grenade launcher?" Paskudnyak asked facetiously. "I hear they're good for an easy kill."

"If you think we need them, I can supply them," Mittenkope said, looking at Boxer.

"What do you think, Stark?" Boxer asked.

"I wasn't thinking of a land war," he answered. "But, to be on the safe side, one might not be a bad idea."

"I was only joking," Paskudnyak said.

Mittenkope shook his head. "When they're angry, nothing about either Shmuh Geh Gee or Fong Shun Un is a joke."

"There's not much about them that's funny when they're not angry," Paskudnyak said.

"One grenade launcher," Boxer told Mittenkope, before Paskudnyak's comments became completely unmanageable.

Mittenkope barked out an order to one of the men standing by, then he said to Boxer, "That's Schmaltz. He's my bastard son, but I can trust him."

Boxer nodded.

"He's going with us," Mittenkope said.

"I thought we were the only ones going," Stark said.

"I just assumed that you would understand that in addition to myself and you people, there would be one or two others that I would take along."

"How many 'one or two others'?" Boxer questioned.

"Well —"

"I don't like that 'well,'" Boxer said.

"Neither do I," Paskudnyak added.

"How many others, Captain?" Boxer pressed.

"Two women and their children."

"Oh?"

"I fathered the children," Mittenkope said proudly. "The girl is three years old, and the boy just half that."

"Well, well, I would have never taken you for the family type," Paskudnyak commented.

Mittenkope drew himself up, and, standing rigidly at attention, he answered, "It is to see my true family that I want to return to the Fatherland."

"True family?" Stark entering the conversation, now asked.

"My wife, Marta, and my children."

Stark wryly said, "I'm amazed at *der Kapitän*'s husbandry."

"Yeah, we'll put it in the *Guinness Book of World Records*," Paskudnyak commented.

Mittenkope broke open another box and took out a 9mm automatic. "Everyone gets one of these and two clips," he said, handing the one in his hand to Stark.

Schmaltz returned with the grenade launcher, armed himself, and, looking more piratical than the rest of them, he seemed to be boyishly pleased with his new weapons.

Mittenkope said, "Now, I will get ready, and then we go." He clicked his heels several times: once in the direction of Stark, whom he seemed to admire more than anyone else, then he clicked his heels at Boxer, at the two women, and finally, though he hesitated, at Paskudnyak.

"Despite the war —"

"Which war?" Boxer asked.

"When a man of my age says 'the war,' he only means one war ... the Second World War, of course," Stark said.

"You know there were a few after that?" Boxer teased.

Stark didn't answer and picked up what he had started to say. "Despite the war, the captain seems to have been a busy man."

"That's because he loves the Fatherland, and what better way to show this love than to contribute to its store of cannon fodder," Paskudnyak said.

"You know what's wrong with you, you have a bad attitude," Stark said.

"Yeah, but it's the kind of bad attitude women love. Isn't that so, Odah?" Paskudnyak asked, grinning at his girlfriend.

"Don't pay any attention to him, Admiral," she said. "His attitude goes beyond being bad. It's downright miserable."

"But lovable... You have to admit that I am lovable," Paskudnyak said.

"Well, maybe —"

"There's no *well* about it —"

Mittenkope returned dressed in his *Kriegsmarine* uniform.

Paskudnyak gave a long low whistle.

Mittenkope smiled appreciatively, and practically pirouetted several times before he said, "Still fits this old man."

"Now, Admiral, you were saying something about my bad attitude?" Paskudnyak questioned gleefully.

Stark glowered at him.

"I don't give a flying fuck what he's wearing, as long as he can get us off this island," Boxer said, annoyed with the two of them.

"We will go now," Mittenkope said, looking at his watch. "The tide will change soon. We'll still have to blast through the sandbar, though."

"That should tell his two sons something," Paskudnyak commented sarcastically. "Even if it doesn't do that, it should wake them up."

Mittenkope didn't respond, but Boxer did. "Captain, we're ready," he said.

"Good. We go. Follow me," Mittenkope told them and started out of the room, with Schmaltz as his point man.

Boxer followed Mittenkope, Stark was next. Then came the two women, Paskudnyak following. Jose was last.

They moved quickly and silently out of the house and to the rear, to a narrow trail, which was barely visible in the dim light of a waning crescent moon.

The trail led directly to the beach, where there was an inflatable large enough to take all of them.

"We will paddle out to that beached tanker over there," Mittenkope shouted above the roar of the surf, the same time gesturing toward a dark hulk that lay off the beach.

Boxer had spotted that wreck when he toured the island, and the other one, an old tramp steamer, about five hundred yards astern of the tanker.

"Getting through this surf isn't going to be easy," Paskudnyak shouted.

Boxer pointed to the inflatable, dropped his weapons into it, and, taking hold of the painter, he waded into the water, pulling the boat after him.

Within moments everyone was pulling the inflatable into the water. Just as they successfully launched it, a sudden blaze of white circles erupted from the hilltop behind them.

"They hit this sucker, and we're shark bait," Paskudnyak shouted, and, grabbing his M-18, he began firing at the searchlights.

Schmaltz and Stark began firing too.

"Get in the boat," Boxer yelled.

Louise and Odah clambered over the rounded gunnels from opposite sides.

"Got one!" Stark yelled.

"There goes another," Jose shouted.

Then the third one was shot out.

"Everyone into the boat," Boxer yelled.

Suddenly, a light machine gun began to spit rounds into the sand, then into the water directly behind them.

"Paddle like hell," Stark told them, firing his M-18 at a point from where the tracers seemed to be coming.

The other men dug their paddles into the water, when suddenly a wave broke over them. The inflatable managed, however, to remain somehow afloat, and the men continued to paddle.

Though wave after wave broke over them, they continued to put distance between themselves and the shore. Finally, they were out of the machine gun's range.

Exhausted, the men paused for a few moments to ease their aching arms and catch their breath.

"We must get to the U-Sixty-nine before my sons do," Mittenkope said.

"I thought they were going to be out for twelve hours," Stark said.

"A normal man would be out that long," Mittenkope said.

"Yeah, but those guys aren't normal," Paskudnyak commented. "They're more like fucking gorillas."

"Let's get to the boat," Boxer said, starting to paddle again.

Minutes later, the inflatable bumped against the rusted stern of the tanker.

"There's a Jacob's ladder midship on the port side," Mittenkope said. "We can work our way to it."

Slowly, they moved to where the rope ladder lay over the side.

"Jose, you go up first," Boxer said.

Jose slung his rifle over his back, and scampered up the ladder, Louise following him, with Odah trailing.

"Captain, you're next," Boxer said. "Stark, you follow him."

In a matter of minutes, everyone was out of the inflatable and on the tanker's deck.

"Well, where's the boat?" Paskudnyak questioned.

"Inside the belly of this hulk," Boxer answered, remembering how the *Shark* — his first command for the Company — could be hidden inside the *Tecumseh*, a supertanker that had been modified to conceal a submarine.

Paskudnyak gave him a questioning look.

"You are correct, Admiral," Mittenkope said, smiling broadly. "But how did you know?"

"It's a long story," Boxer said, "and right now it's unimportant how I knew. But what is important is whether or not your sons know."

"They know," Mittenkope answered. "They will try to stop us. But it will take them some time to get from the cove to where we are."

"How long?" Stark asked.

"The most, an hour."

"And how long will it take us to clear this hulk and be under way?" Paskudnyak asked.

"Once we blow a passageway through the sandbar, we can be under way immediately. We'll be running awash."

"I don't give a damn how we run," Boxer said, "as long as we run."

"Please, follow me," Mittenkope told them. "Be very careful going down the various flights of steps. They are made of wood and have no railings."

They entered the midship cabin, where Mittenkope threw a lever on a huge switchboard that immediately flooded the interior with light. "From a gasoline-driven generator," he said, explaining the source of the power for the lights.

They moved quickly through the cabin and into the tanker's cavernous hold, where a WWII German submarine sat on chocks.

"You mean this first has to be flooded?" Paskudnyak asked.

"Once the steel door is opened, enough water will come in to raise her off the blocks," Mittenkope explained. "We will have four-foot clearance between the boat's keel and the tanker's deck."

"And the propeller, will it clear?" Boxer asked.

"It will," Mittenkope said.

When they finally reached the boat's deck, Schmaltz said, "I go blow sandbar now."

"How long will that take?" Stark asked.

Mittenkope translated the question for his son, who replied in dialect.

"Not more than ten minutes," Mittenkope said. "Once the bar is blown we will refloat the U-Sixty-nine and move her out. Schmaltz will be waiting for us in the inflatable, about two hundred yards ahead."

"Good luck," Boxer said, looking at Schmaltz, who nodded and raced back up the steps.

"We will go into the boat now," Mittenkope said, pointing to the open hatch in the forward section of the deck.

Boxer went down the hatch first and found the boat's interior lighting was on.

Odah followed him, and he helped her down, then Louise.

Mittenkope dropped onto the deck last and shut the hatch cover. Then he said, "Most everything is now automated. I control everything from the bridge — all diving operations — and I set surface and submerged speed. You have the helm, Admiral Boxer. Captain Paskudnyak, you operate all remote controls on my orders."

"Whatever you say," Paskudnyak answered, clicking his heels.

"Cut it out!" Boxer snapped. "If we don't do this right the first time, we won't have a second chance."

"The two women in the forward torpedo room. Admiral Stark, down here on the bridge," Mittenkope said.

Boxer didn't have to ask where he'd be: he knew it would be on the conning tower bridge with Mittenkope.

'Jose and Schmaltz will man the machine guns," Mittenkope said. "Everyone to their stations!" Then he scrambled through the open hatch to the conning tower bridge.

Boxer followed Mittenkope, and, considering the captain's age, he was surprised at the man's agility.

Suddenly there were two loud explosions.

"Schmaltz has done his work," Mittenkope said and pressed two red buttons on a jury-rigged console in front of him.

Instantly, water began to pour out of two twelve-inch diameter pipes, just ahead of the boat's bow.

"Three thousand gallons a minute," Mittenkope shouted above the roar of the incoming water.

"How much time does it take to float her?" Boxer yelled.

"About twelve minutes," Mittenkope answered, again shouting to make himself heard.

Because it was useless to try and carry on a conversation, even a shouting conversation, Boxer nodded and gave his attention over to the various controls on the bridge. But they were either identified with signs in German, or they were completely unmarked. As far as Boxer could make out, there were at least a half-dozen that were not standard equipment.

Suddenly, a slight tremor passed through the U-boat.

Boxer looked at Mittenkope.

He was all smiles. Nodding vigorously, he shouted, "She hasn't been in the water for more than forty years."

Boxer accepted the explanation without comment. He was more concerned with the boat's present operational capabilities, than with her history.

The tremor became stronger.

Boxer checked the lines that secured her to the inside walls of the cargo well. They were taut, but as she rose, they'd become slack and might have to be tightened to prevent the boat from hitting against the inside walls.

"Two feet of water," Mittenkope shouted.

This time Boxer yelled back, "It's looking good."

The U-69's movements became more pronounced; then suddenly she was off the chocks and floating.

Mittenkope cut back on the flow of the water and the roaring sound diminished. "All the external electrical connections are 'quick disconnects,' so that it will be no trouble pulling away from them."

Boxer nodded his head appreciatively. The old man was, in addition to being a very successful pirate, a brilliant engineer.

"As soon as the water level reaches three feet, the outer door will swing open, allowing us access to the sea," Mittenkope said.

"When do we start up the boat's power plant?" Boxer asked.

"Now. Press that red button on the left side of the console."

Boxer pressed the button, and instantly the boat's huge twin diesels sputtered, then began to throb.

"This is the first time in twenty, maybe twenty-five years that they have been switched on," Mittenkope said proudly.

Boxer was tempted to ask if they'd continue to operate, but he knew that such a question would anger the captain, and this was not the time to do that. Even as this thought crossed his mind, the door, or more precisely, the bottom section of the tanker's bow opened.

"We will get under way," Mittenkope pronounced with the absolute authority of the boat's skipper.

Boxer was about to remind him about the two fore and aft lines that secured the boat to the walls of the tanker, when as if he anticipated the question, Mittenkope said, "Once the boat is in motion the strain of the line at the cleat will break it." Then moving his hand to a large control dial, he gave it less than a third of a turn.

The boat's drive shaft was immediately engaged, and the propeller slowly turned over. The U-69 began to move out of the beached tanker, where she'd been cocooned for more than a quarter of century.

She slid easily into a calm sea.

"Gan you see Schmaltz?" Mittenkope asked.

Boxer peered into the darkness, where only a star-studded sky rested on a very black horizon.

"No," Boxer answered, after a few moments.

"We are coming up to the sandbar," Mittenkope said, and he reduced the speed until the U-69 was barely making headway.

Boxer sucked in his breath and waited. If they got hung up on the bar, Fong Shun Un and Shmuh Geh Gee would be able to board.

"Steady as she goes," Mittenkope said.

Boxer relayed the command to Paskudnyak.

"Holding steady as she goes," Paskudnyak answered.

"Depth reading?" Mittenkope asked, then remembering that Boxer wasn't acquainted with the boat's equipment, he switched on the fathometer and said, "Bottom twelve feet." He turned on another piece of electronic gear. "Sonar," he explained. "There's the bar," he said, pointing to the amber screen, where the bottom's topography was clearly visible. "We're moving through it with a bit more than a foot to spare on each side."

The instant the U-69 was through the opening in the sandbar Boxer exhaled.

"Bottom, twenty feet and dropping," Mittenkope said.

Suddenly, a flare exploded white light dead ahead of them.

"Schmaltz!" Mittenkope exclaimed, moving the boat's speed control to full stop and allowing its forward momentum to move it to where Schmaltz was.

"That flare is going to put us in the gunsights of your two sons," Boxer said.

"Schmaltz isn't exactly bright. But he does follow orders."

Boxer didn't answer.

"Ease the helm over to port," Mittenkope said.

Boxer relayed the command to Paskudnyak.

The boat's bow began to swing to the port.

Schmaltz suddenly called out, "Hold steady... I jump!"

And jump he did, from the inflatable to the curve of the boat's ballast tanks. He almost lost his footing, but at the last moment he threw himself forward and grabbed on to the main deck's grating.

Mittenkope gave his attention to the radar screen, which he had activated. "Four MTBs are clearing the cove," he calmly announced. Then, he dialed full speed ahead and ordered the helm onto a different course.

"Those MTBs are closing fast," Boxer said. "Range, fourteen thousand yards."

Mittenkope set his hat on backwards.

Boxer realized that Mittenkope had once again become the U-boat commander that he had been fifty years before.

"All hands, now hear this... All hands, now hear this," Mittenkope said. "All hands battle stations... Battle stations." He rotated the speed control to flank speed, and the U-69 quickly responded.

Boxer watched the radar screen. The MTBs continued to close. "Have they torpedoes?"

"Certainly," Mittenkope snapped. "We bought them fully equipped."

Despite the situation, Boxer voiced his surprise.

"On their mother's side, they have connections to Abbas Mustafa."

Boxer knew the name: Mustafa was the notorious Libyan arms dealer. He sold arms to anyone who had money enough to pay for them.

"Watch the screen," Mittenkope said.

Boxer nodded and looked at the radar display. "They're closing fast," he reported.

Mittenkope checked the screen. "They'll open up with their forties soon," he said.

Boxer replied, "A couple of rounds —" He stopped. The man's eyes had a faraway glazed look. He was somewhere else. Maybe fighting a battle he'd fought during WWII. Boxer switched on the 1MC. "Paskudnyak, we are going to have a real problem if we don't dive."

In ten seconds, Paskudnyak was on the bridge. "What the hell is wrong with him?" he asked, the moment he saw Mittenkope.

"Get him down below," Boxer said, "and make sixty feet."

Paskudnyak hesitated for an instant.

"Do it now," Boxer barked.

Paskudnyak and Schmaltz managed to get Mittenkope through the hatch, while Boxer secured the bridge, closed the hatch, and dogged it.

"Stand by to dive," Boxer shouted, dropping down onto the boat's bridge.

"Dive?" Stark questioned.

"There are four MTBs about two miles away by now, and they're equipped with forties."

Stark gave a slight nod.

Boxer and Paskudnyak worked the various controls that opened the ballast tank valves.

As the forward ballast tanks filled, the bow angled down.

"Too bad we don't know how to control the diving planes," Paskudnyak said.

"She's down twenty now," Boxer said, looking at the depth gauge.

"Those sons of *der Kapitän* will start ranging with their sonar as soon as they realize we went under," Paskudnyak commented.

"Forty feet," Boxer said.

"Do they have ashcans or Subrocs?" Stark asked.

"They bought their MTBs fully equipped from Abbas Mustafa," Boxer answered.

"He deals in state-of-the-art weapons," Paskudnyak said.

"Seventy feet and leveling off," Boxer announced. He vented some ballast and leveled the tanks. "Sixty feet, on the mark," he said.

"Now what?" Stark questioned.

Boxer checked their speed: they were making six knots, which was maximum for the boat. "We're not going to outrun them, and we're no match for them on the surface."

"Fine, that give us only two choices: surface and surrender, or let them kill us down here," Paskudnyak said.

"We have another choice. We can blow them out of the water," Boxer said.

"Torpedoes?" Stark questioned.

"You're counting on —" Paskudnyak said.

"I'm counting on them working. No, I'll start that over again. I'm counting on Mittenkope having kept them in working order."

"Load all four forward tubes," Boxer said, riding the periscope up and turning it in the direction of the oncoming MTBs. "They're fanned out. Stand by to come to course two-five-zero."

"I have the helm," Stark said.

Boxer glanced at him. "This shoot will be off the top of my head." He was used to using computers to solve his fire-control problems. Here, he didn't even have the circular slide rule that was used by boat skippers during World War II.

"Coming to course two-five-zero," Stark answered.

Boxer gave the necessary orders to set the depth and firing mechanisms in the torpedoes.

"Torpedoes running hot," Paskudnyak reported.

"Ranging," Stark said, as the audible pinging from the MTBs resounded through the boat.

Boxer checked the position of the MTBs. "Six thousand yards and closing fast."

Suddenly Mittenkope exclaimed, "Stand by… All hands stand by!"

"Ah shit!" Paskudnyak responded. "What we don't need now is a resurrected Nazi U-boat skipper."

"Schmaltz," Boxer shouted. "Schmaltz, on the bridge."

In moments Schmaltz was there.

"Take care of the captain," Boxer told him. "I don't want him on the bridge now."

Schmaltz nodded, took hold of his father's arm, and began to lead him away.

"I am in command," Mittenkope said, resisting his son. "This is my boat."

Boxer went up to him. "Sorry, Captain," he said and delivered a stunning uppercut to Mittenkope's jaw that sent him crashing to the deck. "Get him off this bridge," Boxer ordered, looking at Schmaltz.

Schmaltz nodded again.

Boxer returned to the periscope. He'd positioned the boat on a 90-degree intercept with the MTBs. "All engines stop," he said.

Paskudnyak stopped the boat's engines.

"Fire one," Boxer ordered.

A sudden hissing filled the boat and the vessel rose slightly.

"Fire two," Boxer said.

"Two away," Jose called out.

Boxer went to the periscope. The MTBs were still holding their course. Boxer sucked in his breath. Then suddenly he saw the wake of one of the torpedoes. At the same time the MTB on the near flank started to turn. But the maneuver was seconds too late. The torpedo struck and the boat became an orange-red ball of flame, while the sound of the explosion pounded down on the U-69.

The remaining three boats began to execute a full 90-degree turn.

The second torpedo slammed into one of the boats, holed her, but failed to explode.

Boxer reported the action as he saw it.

"There's still two more MTBs up there," Stark said.

"One is picking up survivors and the other is heading back to the cove," Boxer answered. He lowered the periscope, and, using a handkerchief, he wiped the sweat from his brow. "Our best bet is to stay down until darkness, surface, and get the hell out of here."

"How much water do we have under us?" Paskudnyak asked.

Boxer found the fathometer controls and turned it on. "One hundred and fifty feet... But all around us the depth goes down to three thousand feet."

"Lucky us," Stark said.

"Okay, let's go to the bottom and stay there for the next few hours," Boxer said.

"Going down," Paskudnyak called out as he flooded the ballast tanks.

CHAPTER 6

"Was it really necessary to hit me so hard?" Mittenkope asked, rubbing his jaw. He was stretched out on the bunk in the small captain's quarters.

"I should have hit you harder," Boxer answered. "Bad enough that you tell us about the fully equipped MTBs when they are chasing us, but you conveniently forgot to tell us about your lapses into —"

"I cannot tell you everything, at least not all at once," Mittenkope said as he sat up.

"Hit him again," Paskudnyak demanded. "If you don't, I will."

Boxer waved him silent and said, "Captain, we're sitting on the bottom, resting on the top of a small undersea mountain whose base is three thousand feet down."

"And the MTBs?" Mittenkope asked.

"One sunk, a second holed and left sinking, and two still completely operational."

"We must make them think we're sunk," Mittenkope said. "We will release oil and fire some debris into the water from the torpedo tubes." He stood up. "If Fong Shun Un thinks we're alive, he'll come after us." He looked at Schmaltz, who was standing by, and spoke to him in the island dialect. "He will take care of it," Mittenkope assured them.

"There's the matter of the charts," Paskudnyak said. "I'd like to see them. In fact, I think we should have them, just in case the captain takes another, and a longer trip into the twilight zone and doesn't make it back."

Boxer had already decided that in his eagerness to get off the island, he had allowed himself and the others to be duped, and now was as good a time as any to say so. But Mittenkope spoke first. "The charts are in the safe behind you, Admiral Boxer. If you will move aside, I will open the safe."

Boxer was willing to play along and stepped aside.

Mittenkope smiled, went to the safe, and without any hesitation dialed in the combination. On his first try, the safe opened, and he removed two charts that had been rolled into cylinders. "One of these will show my daily position from the time I left my base in Kiel to the time I first spotted the *Edinburgh* and began to track her, and the second chart marks her position in relation to significant land and sea positions."

"Did you know what she was carrying before you sank her?" Boxer asked.

He nodded, then he said, "I don't know how we knew, but we did." Then he unrolled the first chart. "We were three days into the patrol when the message came that the *Edinburgh* was in our sector and must be sunk, even if it required ramming her."

Frowning, Boxer studied the chart for several moments, then he said, "Unroll the other one, Captain."

Mittenkope obliged.

After a few moment's study, Boxer said, "The coordinates are not the same."

Mittenkope grinned. "Ah, so you saw that so quickly. During the war, the *Kriegsmarine* used Berlin for its zero longitude. This one has my check positions based on Berlin, the other one on the standard, Greenwich, England."

"How do we know that any of this is real?" Paskudnyak asked.

"But the charts show it," Mittenkope said.

"Jack —"

"We don't know and what is more we won't know until we use the charts to find the wreck. If they're accurate, then we will find the wreck."

"You will find her where it is marked on the chart," Mittenkope assured them.

"You can roll up the charts now," Boxer said. "Now we have to concentrate on getting the hell out of here."

Paskudnyak checked his watch, then said, "I'm going to get some sack time."

"Good idea," Boxer said. He had decided to sleep on the bridge, where he could immediately take charge should a situation arise that demanded it. Then, turning to Mittenkope, he asked, "Do we have provisions on board? Things like coffee, milk, and canned goods?"

"Certainly," Mittenkope responded. "There is even a store of frozen meat, chicken, and fish on board. I prepared the U-Sixty-nine for a long voyage home."

"Suppose we have Jose whip up something to eat," Boxer said, "and then all of us will get some z's and be wide awake when we surface tonight."

"That's more than eight hours away," Mittenkope said.

Boxer shrugged. "Right now, I'm in a rush. I've had enough excitement for one day. I'm sure we'll have more tonight."

"I'll tell Jose to get to work," Paskudnyak said.

"Tell Schmaltz to help him," Mittenkope suggested. "Schmaltz is as good as any gourmet cook."

Paskudnyak rolled his eyes and left.

"Now tell me, Captain, about your spells," Boxer said.

Mittenkope shrugged his shoulders. "It doesn't happen often," he said, "and they never last too long."

"I'm sure there is some sort of medication you can take that will help you," Boxer told him.

"I have medication, but I don't like taking pills. I don't even like going to a doctor."

Boxer didn't answer. He himself had the same attitude toward doctors and pills.

"So you got one of the MTBs," Mittenkope said, his voice full of admiration.

"Lucky shot," Boxer answered.

"Lucky, but filled with experience."

"That too."

Mittenkope went to a small closet and, opening it, said, "I still have some schnapps left from the old days." And he took out a bottle half-filled with a deep brown liquid. "We drink to your 'lucky shot,' and to the great good luck that brought us together." He handed the bottle to Boxer. I have shot glasses here, too. Unless you prefer to drink from the bottle."

"The bottle will do," Boxer said, accepting Mittenkope's challenge and offer of friendship. He opened the bottle and toasted, "To Lady Luck, may she always be close to us." Then he drank. The liquid slid smoothly down his throat and immediately burst into a delightful feeling of warmth that spread rapidly through his body.

"After I see my real family and settle down," Mittenkope said, "I will write a book about my adventures. I should have already written it, but the closing chapters, I always knew, would have to be about recovering the gold from the *Edinburgh*."

Boxer helped himself to a second drink. "This is good stuff," he commented.

"The best… It came from Hitler's private stock. He gave me the bottle just before I left on my last patrol."

That he was standing there drinking schnapps with a former German U-boat skipper who had known Hitler seemed to be almost a crazy dream to Boxer. It was as if something of the past had suddenly intruded itself in the present. And the fact that the surroundings were completely the 1940s made it seem even more surrealistic.

"He was a very generous man," Mittenkope said.

"Who?"

"Hitler."

"Generous, no doubt, to a fault," Boxer responded sarcastically.

"He —"

"He was one of history's all-time monsters," Boxer finished for him.

Mittenkope poured himself a second drink. "I grant you he did some very bad things, but —"

Boxer shook his head. "With all due respect to whatever you think, the man is not one of my favorite historical figures. He ranks, in my mind, a close second to Caligula."

"'Judge not, lest ye be judged.' Isn't that —"

"Just a word of advice, Captain. Never, never voice your views about Hitler when Captain Paskudnyak is anywhere in hearing distance."

"Why?"

"He'd probably kill you," Boxer answered in a flat, hard voice.

Several moments passed before Mittenkope said, "I'll remember that." Then, he finished his drink.

Boxer put his empty glass down on the small, gray desk bolted to the bulkhead, thanked him for the drinks, and went straight to the bridge, where he found Stark waiting for him. "The charts appear to be genuine," he said.

"Paskudnyak told me," Stark answered.

"She's down in eight hundred feet of water," Boxer told him.

"I don't think the depth will be a problem; we have submersibles that operate at much greater depths, but the currents there will be."

"I know. I've been there."

"One problem at a time," Stark said.

Boxer looked around, then commented, "Don't you have the feeling that you've been somehow thrown back in time?"

"If you mean that being here feels like the 'Twilight Zone,' the answer is, yes, it certainly does."

They looked at one another, smiled, then laughed.

"Get some sleep," Boxer said.

"What about you?"

"I'll manage to sleep here."

"On the deck?"

"It's good for the back. Besides, unless there's a woman in it, a bed is just another place," Boxer said, knowing that the comment would get a rise out of Stark.

"You know, I really think you're sick," Stark responded.

"Certainly I am. 'I'm sick for the love of a maid'," Boxer croaked off-key.

"You're —"

Suddenly, a shudder passed through the boat.

"What the hell was that?" Stark asked.

Boxer went to 1MC, switched it on, and said, "All hands, all hands, stand by... Paskudnyak and Captain Mittenkope report to the bridge on the double."

The boat shuddered again.

"I think a major problem is developing."

Mittenkope and Paskudnyak arrived at the same moment.

"Captain —"

Another shudder passed through the boat.

"Too deep," Mittenkope said. "We are too deep. The repairs made —"

Simultaneously Boxer, Stark, and Paskudnyak reached the same conclusion and began to speak at the same time. But it was Stark's voice that prevailed. "She was never tested, was she?"

Mittenkope shook his head. "Only awash," he answered.

"Blow negative!" Boxer said tightly.

Paskudnyak ran to the dive controls.

"Do the diving planes work?" he asked, looking directly at Mittenkope.

The man nodded.

"When I tell you to, give me maximum angle up."

"Yes, Admiral," Mittenkope responded and went to the wheel controls.

Boxer called the women to the bridge over 1MC. "Louise, stand next to the captain. Move the wheel in front of you exactly as he moves the wheel in front of him. Odah, you watch that panel of lights, and if any one of them should go from green to red, let me know immediately," Boxer said, pointing to the scram panel located on the bulkhead over the doorway leading to the forward part of the boat.

Air suddenly began to hiss.

Boxer started the engine, going to ahead, full power. The boat suddenly trembled, began to rise, and moved forward.

"Maximum up on diving planes," Boxer said, watching the inclinometer. The boat's bow was slowly responding. His eyes went to the depth gage. They were moving through two hundred feet.

Suddenly, the boat's plates began to groan. Two rivets popped, making shotlike sounds.

"Red light!" Odah exclaimed.

"Mittenkope, what's the scram board?" Boxer shouted, dropping the "Captain."

"A problem in the battery room," he said.

"What kind of a problem?" Boxer asked, exasperated by the captain's vagueness.

"Sea water —"

"Seal off battery room," Boxer ordered.

Paskudnyak ran from the diving room to the battery room, where the greenish colored chlorine gas was already lying close to the floor.

"Battery-room door shut and sealed off," Paskudnyak shouted.

The boat was making a slow ascent.

Another green light went to red on the scram board.

"Not enough air pressure —"

Boxer shook his head. "Don't fucking tell me," he exploded.

Ignoring Boxer's outburst, Mittenkope reported, "The main air compressor has malfunctioned."

"We're still a hundred feet down," Boxer said.

"We might get another fifty feet out of her," Stark offered.

Boxer nodded. "We're going to get rid of everything we don't need."

Paskudnyak, Stark, and Mittenkope immediately understood, and headed for the torpedo room. In a matter of minutes they had fired the remaining torpedoes, and anything else they could stuff into the torpedo tubes.

The U-69 gained another sixty feet. Its snorkel was now above water. This permitted Boxer to disengage the electric motors and switch to diesel power. The boat plowed along at eighteen knots, while Paskudnyak continued to nudge her closer to the surface.

After several minutes another ten feet was gained. The radio mast was now out of the water.

Boxer set Stark and Mittenkope to the task of radioing for help.

Suddenly, one of the seams just beyond the bridge opened and water began to pour into the boat.

"Stark, did you get anyone?" Boxer shouted.

"We can't receive," Stark answered.

"We're abandoning ship. Send that... Give our position, then come back to the bridge. We're going out on Momsen Lungs through the forward hatch," Boxer yelled.

"Jack, she's beginning to drift down," Paskudnyak said.

Boxer checked the depth gauge: she was down twenty-five feet. He glanced at the women. They looked terrified.

"Put the lungs on the women," Boxer told Stark. "You go out first, they'll follow. Paskudnyak next. Mittenkope after him. Jose, then Schmaltz. I'll be the last."

"By that time the boat will be down another fifty feet," Stark said.

Boxer shrugged.

"One more try," Paskudnyak said and opened the control valve to blow the main ballast.

They all heard a hiss, then suddenly Boxer saw the needle on the depth gauge begin to quiver.

"It's moving," Stark whispered, then louder, "By God, we're moving up."

Boxer put all engines, "ahead full power."

The U-69's bow angle increased.

"She's going to surface," Jose yelled.

"Stand by to open the forward hatch," Boxer ordered.

"Standing by," Paskudnyak answered.

"Twenty-five feet, ten ... open the hatch," Boxer yelled.

Paskudnyak undogged the hatch and flung it open. Water poured down into the boat.

Boxer cut the boat's speed to zero.

"Two inflatables in the conning tower, alongside the deck door," Mittenkope said.

"Jose, you and Schmaltz get those inflatables and launch them," Boxer said. "Everyone else, on deck, now."

The boat began to slow, and as it slowed, it also drifted lower.

Boxer ran back to the captain's room, took the two charts that showed the *Edinburgh*'s position, and dashed back to the open hatchway. Moments later he was on the deck and saw that Paskudnyak and the two women were in one inflatable, while Stark and the other men were in the other. The boat's forward movement had already moved him some distance from the inflatables.

"There's room here," Louise yelled.

"Here, catch!" Boxer shouted and tossed the two charts to her. As soon as she caught them, he dove over the side and started swimming toward the rubber raft.

"She's beginning to sink," Paskudnyak yelled.

Boxer looked over his right shoulder. The U-69 was awash, dead in the water. Then suddenly her stern began to rise out of the water, and, with a strange, almost gasping sound, she slipped under the water, bow first.

Boxer glanced over at Mittenkope. The man was on his feet, his hand raised in a silent salute to his boat.

"Come aboard," Paskudnyak called as he paddled closer to Boxer.

A few minutes later, Boxer was safely on the rubber raft. "Well," he said, "those of you who pray, better start praying that we're rescued before Fong Shun Un and Shmuh Geh Gee find us." The moment he stopped speaking, the bright blue sky seemed to explode with the roaring sound of choppers.

There were three of them with red, white, and blue markings and *Navy* printed in big blue letters on their fuselages.

"Now that's what I call good timing," Boxer yelled above the choppers' roar.

CHAPTER 7

"Now, let me get this straight, you intend to salvage the gold?" William C. Kahn, the director of the CIA, asked, his pale blue eyes riveted on Boxer.

"You got it straight," Boxer answered. He, Stark, Paskudnyak and Mittenkope had spent the last hour and a half recounting what had happened to them over the last few days. Kahn had listened without interrupting, but now he was primed for action. Boxer knew all the signs: body bent forward, elbows planted on the desk, and forearms almost vertical.

"I may have it straight, but you can't do it without my permission," Kahn said, obviously relishing the power he had.

"You're joking."

"And furthermore, Captain Paskudnyak, from what the CNO has told me, will soon be reassigned to another billet. And as for your Captain Mittenkope, he's nothing but a pirate, and if I have anything to say about it, he will be tried as one and hopefully executed."

"That leaves me," Stark said angrily.

"With all due respects, Admiral, even at your age, I would choose better companions," Kahn said.

"And with no respect, I suggest that you pay strict attention to what Admiral Boxer has to say," Stark shot back.

Kahn winced.

"We're talking about four hundred and fifty million dollars' worth of gold when its price was set at thirty-five dollars an ounce. Now that same gold has a market value in the billions. I'm going after it, and there is nothing you can do to stop me. I'm going to go to the Russians. I'm sure they'll cooperate."

"You can't do that!" Kahn shouted, leaping to his feet.

"Watch me," Boxer answered.

Just then the phone on Kahn's desk rang. He answered with a gruff, "What is it, now?" Then he listened for a few moments. "Send him right in," he said. Putting the phone down, he announced that Admiral Samuel Pierce, the Chief of Naval Operations and head of the Joint Chiefs of Staff, had arrived.

"You can bring the President here," Boxer said, "and that won't change my plans."

The door opened, and Admiral Pierce entered. He was a tall, dignified man with pepper-and-salt hair.

Boxer and Paskudnyak saluted him, and he returned the courtesy.

Stark shook his hand, then gesturing toward Mittenkope, he introduced him.

Mittenkope stood up, snapped to attention, and saluted.

The CNO momentarily looked bewildered, then saluted.

"You had quite an adventure, didn't you," the CNO commented as he pulled a chair into the semicircle in front of Kahn's desk and sat down.

"It was interesting," Stark answered.

"Well, I'm happy that none of you became casualties," Pierce said.

"All of us were damn close to becoming casualties," Boxer replied. "We just managed to abandon the captain's boat before she dove into the deep six for good."

"Let's stop the chitchat for now and get down to the problem at hand," Kahn said.

"There isn't any problem," Boxer responded, "at least not from where I sit. What about you, Stark, do you see a problem?"

"No."

"Paskudnyak?"

"No."

"And I happen to know that Captain Mittenkope doesn't see one either," Boxer said.

"They want to engage in a salvage operation," Kahn said.

Boxer quickly explained the what and the why of the operation.

Then Kahn said, "We can't have our people off on their own operations, no matter who they are and what the operation might be worth."

Boxer considered that for a moment, then he said, "Okay, you're right."

"Well, I'm glad to hear you finally say that," Kahn told him.

"We'll do it under government sponsorship — this government and the Soviets — and a cut of the final take."

"What?"

"Twenty-five percent will do fine," Boxer said.

"But you're already a multimillionaire —"

"What I am or am not worth doesn't happen to be any of your business."

Kahn ignored his jibe and started to say something about the Russians, but Boxer interrupted and said, "It was their gold to begin with."

"We can't be sure of that," Pierce said.

"Deal or no deal?" Boxer finally challenged, tired of the negotiations.

"I must have time to think about this," Kahn said.

"Absolutely. We need more time," Pierce echoed.

"Sorry, gentlemen, time has run out. I will contact the Soviet —"

"You can't," Kahn told him.

"Oh yes, I'm a private citizen," Boxer said. "I was relieved of my command prior to my leaving in the *Sea Dog*," Boxer said. "I only came here first out of courtesy and my feeling of loyalty to my country."

"I wouldn't exactly say you displayed any of those feelings here today," Kahn responded.

Again Boxer addressed Kahn and Pierce as gentlemen, then he said, "Either you give me an answer — and that means the absolute command of operation — now, or I go to the Soviets and present them with the same deal."

"You wouldn't!" Pierce exclaimed.

"Oh, but I would," Boxer answered without hesitation.

Suddenly, Mittenkope cleared his throat, and all eyes went to him, but he looked only at Boxer. "These men are fools, Admiral, and I don't have so much time left that I can waste it on fools."

"You're right, Captain," Boxer answered.

"And," Mittenkope began again, "if I know my son, Fong Shun Un, he's not going to rest until he comes after the gold."

"Fong Shun Un is your son?" Kahn questioned, his voice rising several tones above its normal range.

With fatherly pride, Mittenkope answered, "He is, and so is Shmuh Geh Gee."

"I can't believe I'm holding a conference, not only with one of the world's worst pirates, but also the father of two of the most wanted men in the world."

"Not the worst pirate," Mittenkope corrected, "but the best, the most successful."

Kahn uttered a noisy exasperation.

Then, Mittenkope smiled. "My sons and I chewed up men like you, *Herr Direktor*, and spat them out. Now, if you will excuse me, I will take my charts to more reasonable men."

"Maybe we should get to the President on this one?" Pierce suggested.

"You have twenty-four hours," Boxer said. "You know the hotel I stay at." He stood up. "I don't have anything else to say."

"I can't speak your damn language and you can't speak mine, so you do the best you can with English," Abbas Mustafa said, looking up at Fong Shun Un and Shmuh Geh Gee. "Now, I know about the gold, and I know about Boxer and the rest of them, so you can start by telling me how we can steal the charts and get the gold for ourselves."

Fong Shun Un's brow wrinkled. He marveled that the man seated behind the big polished desk was so fucking stupid. "No steal charts," he finally said.

"All right, 'no steal charts' — but if 'no steal charts,' how do we get gold?"

"Get gold from ship?" Fong Shun Un said.

"All right, we'll dance your way. How do we get the gold from ship?"

"Take it," Fong Shun Un said. "Dive, kill all other divers," he said, flicking his fingers into a closed, then open fist to emphasize his point. "They dive, we dive too. On the bottom, we have big fight. We win. We take gold."

Abbas Mustafa nodded, picked up the phone, punched out a number, waited a moment, and as soon as he heard the voice on the other end, he said, speaking in Arabic, "You sent me a couple of fucking nuts, Yazid. I think you're smoking too much —"

"Mustafa, did I ever lead you astray? I'll admit the two of them are a bit weird, even for my tastes —"

"You sleeping with their sister, or —"

"Nah, years ago, when their mother was young and very beautiful, I made it with her a few times, then one day she was either pissed at something or got so carried away giving me head, that she bit me."

"What?" Mustafa laughed.

"Yeah, she bit. By the beard of Allah, I thought she had part of it, and that I wasn't left with very much of it."

Mustafa exploded with laughter. He was a fat man and the loose flowing white robe he wore accentuated his quivering body.

Fong Shun Un did not like it when someone laughed without telling him why. It always made him uneasy. He looked at his brother, and, in the dialect of the island, he said, "Maybe I should cut his throat?"

"Mama wouldn't like it... Her friend Yazid wouldn't like it."

Fong Shun Un didn't answer.

"Stop laughing," Yazid said.

"That's a funny story," Mustafa replied as he wiped the tears from his eyes.

"Funny now, not so funny then," Yazid answered. "Now listen to me, you let those two excuses for human beings do what they want to do to get the gold. When they have it, my men will be there to take it from them."

Mustafa stopped laughing. "They'll do all the work —"

"I was wondering how long it would take you to catch on."

"It's going to cost," Mustafa said.

"Not as much as you might think. I'll put the equipment package together myself. You take care of everything else."

"All right, you have a deal. By the way, who else is cut into this pie?"

"A few of our friends. It doesn't matter who they are now. Later we'll worry about who gets what. Now, it's just the two of us."

Mustafa didn't like the vagueness of Yazid's answers, but he had many dealings with the man and knew him to be honest, which was probably more than he could say for most of his other business associates.

"By the way, how is the weather in Tripoli?" Yazid asked.

"Not too bad. How is it in Hong Kong?"

"Hot and humid."

Mustafa glanced over at his two guests. Speaking into the phone again, he said, "I'd better get off now. The old one looks as if he's ready to cut my balls off."

"Don't fool yourself. If he looks that way, you can bet that he'll do it."

"Thanks for sending me these two animals."

"Golden animals," Yazid laughed and clicked off.

Mustafa turned toward Fong Shun Un and Shmuh Geh Gee and said, "Tell me exactly what you will need to recover the gold."

"How much you want?" Fong Shun Un asked.

"Sixty percent," Mustafa answered, giving the first number that came into his head.

"Shmuh Geh Gee, we waste our time," Fong Shun Un said. "We go find other money. Arab money come too high." He was on his feet and started for the door, his brother following close behind him.

"Wait a minute," Mustafa called. "That was only an opening number."

'It closing number too. We go," Fong Shun Un said, his hand already on the doorknob.

Abbas Mustafa somehow managed to make his huge bulk move, and he stood up, saying, "It's always better to have a bird in the hand than two in the bush."

Fong Shun Un looked at his brother. "What that mean?"

Shmuh Geh Gee shrugged. "Tell him we no talk about birds."

"We not talk about birds," Fong Shun Un said.

"You no talk about birds, right, but I'm your big bird," Mustafa said. "I have the money you need."

"Get money from different big bird," Fong Shun Un said. "This big bird vulture."

Mustafa roared with laughter. "That's funny, very funny. I have to remember to use that line... I like men who have a sense of humor."

"No like man who laughs," Fong Shun Un said. "Go find money —"

"Come back and sit down," Mustafa said, waving them toward the chairs they had occupied. "There isn't anything that can't be worked out. I am sure we can find a way. Besides, gentlemen, my cousin Yazid would be very upset if we did not work something out, and I know your mother would also be upset."

Speaking in their own dialect, Fong Shun Un said to Shmuh Geh Gee, "It's hard enough to deal with Mama the way it is. I don't want to make her angry."

Shmuh Geh Gee nodded. "The last time she became angry at me, I had to hide out for three weeks."

"Okay, we sit and talk," Fong Shun Un said, letting go of the doorknob and starting back to the desk.

Mustafa sat down and smiled at the two gorillas in front of him. He had already decided to steal the charts from Boxer. Fong Shun Un and his brother were just backup, in case the plan failed. And even if they did finally get the gold, they wouldn't live to enjoy it. No, these two excuses for human beings were two birds in his hand, and what made it so enjoyable was the fact that they didn't even know it.

The bargaining began and Mustafa loved every minute of it. He became the Arab trader of old, haggling over the price of a block of salt or a rug in a bazaar that could have been anywhere in the Arab world. It was a joy. It was invigorating to play this wonderful game percentage point by percentage point.

But Fong Shun Un and Shmuh Geh Gee had dealt with this kind of haggling all of their lives and knew that the man who had the greatest staying power always won.

By the time the bargaining was over, Abbas Mustafa was willing to accept twenty-two and a half percent, with no escalation clauses in the agreement. To his surprise, the two men sitting in front of the desk proved more than a match for him. All his good feelings vanished, and, humiliated, he accepted the twenty-two and a half percent.

The deal was sealed with a handshake, and as Fong Shun Un and Shmuh Geh Gee left the office, Fong Shun Un said, "If the charts are stolen from our father, we will come back and cut your balls off and make you eat them raw."

Mustafa managed a smile. "I certainly don't want that to happen," he said.

"Good, then maybe it won't," Fong Shun Un said as he closed the door, leaving Mustafa to think about the word *maybe*.

Kahn lit a cigar, left his desk, and paced back and forth, leaving a trail of blue-gray smoke hanging in the air above him. "I'm not about to let Boxer get his hands on that gold," he said.

"I don't think you can do anything about it," Admiral Pierce said. "He's not answerable to you anymore."

Kahn stopped. "Do you really think he'll go to the Russians?" he asked.

"If he says he will, he will," Pierce answered.

Kahn pointed his cigar at the admiral, "Why is Boxer always in the center of the worst scenario that I can imagine?"

Pierce contained a smile and said, "It's more coincidence than anything planned."

"Imagine if I believed in luck," the head of the Company said.

"I suggest that we finance the operation, or better still permit the Russians to pick up half the tab. After all, they'll probably start yelling about having the right to either salvage it themselves or want a major share of it."

"I hate like hell to give in to that son-of-a-bitch," Kahn said.

"Let the Russians in and you take away his leverage."

"*Yeah*... Oh, I like that" Kahn said with a smile. "Then he'll have to play it our way."

"Never count on that."

"The Russians aren't going to take to Captain Mittenkope," Kahn said gleefully.

"Let Boxer worry about that," Pierce said.

Kahn sat down. "Okay, we let the Russians know, and we give Boxer the go ahead. For once, I'd like to see him get caught in the stew. Just once!"

CHAPTER 8

Boxer returned to his hotel room, and just as he stretched out on the bed, the phone rang. He was tempted not to pick it up, but after the fourth ring, he did, and said, "Boxer here."

With laughter in her voice, the woman mimicked him. "Brennan here."

"I don't know you," Boxer said, trying to hide the amusement in his voice.

"That's something I want to correct," she answered.

"When?"

"In about twenty minutes."

"Where?"

"There's a party on the fifth floor of the hotel. In fact, there are many parties. The ABA —"

"I don't like patriotic organizations."

She laughed and said, "The American Book Association."

"Still sounds patriotic to me," Boxer responded.

"Believe me, except for the word *American*, it has nothing to do with patriotism. It's wholly devoted to the furtherment of the capitalistic pursuits of its member publishers."

"Ah, why didn't you say so in the first place?" Boxer said.

"I can see that we'll get on real well," she laughed.

"Okay, you've convinced me," Boxer said, then he added, "At the risk of being crude, what's in it for me?"

For a moment, she was silent. "From what little I know about you, I would have made book on the fact that you are a gambler."

"Only when the odds are so great that my life or the lives of others hangs in the balance of my choice."

"You wouldn't consider gambling for any other stakes?" she asked.

"Name them."

She laughed. "Come, come, Admiral, I'm sure you're smart enough to know that you wouldn't be left empty-handed, so to speak."

"It's beginning to sound interesting," Boxer said.

"To find out just how interesting, why don't you come to the party, room five-oh-nine."

"How will I know you?"

"I know you," she answered and clicked off.

Boxer put the phone down, went into the bathroom, washed his face, and took a moment to look at himself in the mirror. His face, tanned from the tropical sun, seemed younger, but his age, and eons more, were lodged in his gray eyes, though at a casual glance a stranger could easily interpret what he saw as an indication of boredom, or perhaps even dissatisfaction.

"Well, well, Jack," he said aloud, "such introspection is bad for the karma, especially when I'm on my way to meet a strange and beautiful — I hope she's beautiful — woman." And having said that, he left the bathroom, and moments later he was out of the room, on his way to room 509.

There was a genuine party going on in the room, which turned out to be a suite of four rooms. There were several other parties in progress in the nearby suites.

The party in 509 was given by Zulu Books, a paperback house with a varied line that ranged from Westerns to true adventure. Boxer learned this just by looking at some of the promotional material taped onto the walls or standing on large, but very flimsy-looking easels.

The place was crowded, noisy, and surprisingly free of smoke. Waiters offered a variety of drinks and hot and cold hors d'oeuvres. And there were two bars set up: one in the foyer area and one in the sitting room, into which he moved.

Boxer went to the bar and ordered vodka on the rocks. "Stoli, if you have it."

The barkeep said, "Only the house brand."

Boxer made a face. "Is the scotch the house brand too?"

The man nodded.

"I'll go for the vodka," Boxer said.

"I'm Horace Keen," a man announced as he fell in alongside of Boxer.

Boxer made a half-turn to his right. The man next to him was short, heavyset, and balding. His fingernails were manicured, and he wore a hound's-tooth jacket, black baggy pants, and a white shirt open at the neck.

"Drink, sir," the barkeep said.

Boxer picked up the glass, nodded to the man, then acknowledged Keen by also nodding to him.

"Scotch... Make it a double," Keen told the barkeeper. Then, in the same breath, he asked, "What do you write?"

"Reports when I have to," Boxer answered, wondering what was keeping Ms. Brennan from making her appearance.

"That's my book, over there. That hideous-looking cover that these cheap bastards blew up to poster size."

"*Passion's Players*," Boxer said, reading the title.

Keen nodded, then laughed. Taking his double scotch from the bar, he said, "What the fuck, it pays the bills."

"Nothing wrong with that," Boxer said, suddenly spotting a woman with long red hair coming toward him.

Keen saw her too and said, "Now that's the kind of woman I'd like for Christmas, or for that matter, any time."

She was wearing a red form-fitting, off-the-shoulder dress, complemented by a blue silk shawl trimmed with elaborate white stitching.

"Know who she is?" Keen asked in a conspiratorial whisper.

"No, but I'm sure that in a matter of moments her ID will have been established," Boxer whispered back.

The woman's red lips suddenly smiled, and when she was still a yard away from the two men, she said, "Admiral Boxer, I presume?" And thrust out her hand.

Boxer joined his to hers and said, "Ms. Brennan, I'm sure."

Both of them laughed, and she said, "Kate, to be less formal, Admiral."

"Jack... My friends call me Jack."

"You're Admiral Boxer?" Keen asked, unable to hide his astonishment. "Admiral Jack Boxer?"

Boxer nodded.

"Are you going to write a book about your experiences in the South China Sea?" Keen asked.

"No, I am going to write it for him," Kate answered, her blue eyes alight with laughter, though she kept a straight face.

To Boxer's complete surprise, she somehow maneuvered herself to his side and possessively entwined her arm around his. Now he was sure she wasn't wearing much of anything under that sheath. He could feel the warm press of her left breast against his arm.

"I hope not for Zulu," Keen responded. "That's if you expect to be paid sometime in the reasonable future."

Curious, Boxer asked, "What's reasonable?"

"Oh, between now and then," Keen replied. "*Then* being Eastern Future Time."

Boxer laughed, so did Kate.

"It's worse if you earn any royalties," Keen said. "Then *now* becomes linked to Ravina's menstrual cycle, and *then* is linked to whistling Dixie, if you know what I mean."

"Who's Ravina?" Boxer questioned.

"She's the owner," Kate answered. "This is not a publicly owned company."

"Strictly a mom-and-pop operation," Keen said.

"Should I know who Pop is, just in case I bump into him this evening?" Boxer asked.

"It doesn't matter," Kate said, "I don't intend to write our book for this company. They'll never pay the advance we want."

Boxer looked at her. "I'm glad you know so much about these things, because this part of your *we* doesn't know diddly."

Without a blink, Kate replied, "The less you know, the happier you will be."

"On that note," Boxer said, "I'm not so sure that I have the necessary credentials to play this game." And disentangling himself from Kate's arm, he added, "I'm crazy, but I'll have to wait some to be as crazy as you appear to be. Now, if you'll excuse me, I've had a difficult day, and I would like to spend the rest of the evening in a quiet atmosphere." He nodded to each of them and headed straight out of the room, toward the door.

Moments later, Boxer was in an elevator on his way down to the lobby and the restaurant where he was known.

The maître d', Paul Entremont, welcomed him with a smile and a handshake, then he escorted him to his favorite table, in the far corner, where the light was dimmest.

Boxer ordered another vodka, and this time he got a Stoli, and by the time it was brought to him, he was deep in thought about the technical aspect of the salvage operation. No matter what decision came from Kahn and Pierce, he decided to drive down to Stark's place and get his input on the plans.

The waiter came to the table, handed him a red leatherbound menu and took a moment to recite the specials of the day.

Boxer politely listened to the waiter's spiel, then he said, "I'll have the Oysters Rockefeller, vegetable and barley soup, and an end cut of prime rib, well done, please."

The waiter acknowledged the order with a nod, then he asked if Boxer wanted another drink.

"Yes, but there is no hurry. I still have this to work on," he said, lifting the glass in front of him.

"Yes, sir," the waiter responded and left the table.

Boxer returned to thinking about the salvage operation, but now, for some unknown reason, he wasn't able to concentrate on it, and, despite his attempt to fight it off, he was becoming more and more depressed. He'd been through a number of post-operation depressions to know that they were normal and only lasted a short time. But he remembered that he was in something of a funk before he and Stark started their round-the-world cruise.

His life, as far as he could tell, was, though full of adventure, not much different from the lives of most people. He had his pack of troubles to carry like anyone else. He'd lost people near and dear to him, and rode the emotional roller coaster of love more times than he cared to remember. But now, when he should be able to enjoy himself, he would soon be off again, risking his life for something that had no real value to him. He had already decided that the money he'd gain would go to several charities.

The waiter brought another Stoli just as Boxer finished the one he had been drinking.

"You can bring the oysters," Boxer told him. Suddenly, he had lost his appetite and wondered how he would manage to eat even half the food he'd ordered.

"Is anything wrong?" the waiter asked.

"Suppose you give me the bill. I'm not really hungry."

"Are you sure?"

"I'm sure," Boxer said.

The waiter sighed and left the table to prepare the bill, while Boxer continued to drink the Stoli. That someone wanted to write a book about his latest adventure, he suddenly found amusing, and it was even more amusing when he thought about Kate actually doing it. Boxer considered himself a private person, a self-contained person, and the idea of him opening up to some strange woman made the whole idea even funnier.

The waiter returned with the check, and Boxer used a credit card to pay for it. He left the restaurant and started for the elevator with the thought that he'd return to his room, but he changed his mind. He crossed the lobby, and, using the revolving door, he stepped out onto the street.

He took a few moments to fill and light his pipe, then he stepped off at a brisk pace. Walking always helped him recover his balance whenever he was depressed or wrestling with what at the time appeared to be an insoluble problem.

Boxer knew he had a problem, but he also knew that he couldn't define it; and if he couldn't do that, there wasn't any way he could solve it.

He walked several blocks before he realized he'd entered one of the all too numerous slum areas in the nation's capital. He stopped in the middle of the block. When he turned around and started walking back, he saw them: three young men, two Hispanic, and one Black. They wore the uniform of the street, the obligatory black leather jacket, torn jeans, a colored bandanna tied around a black belt, and very expensive sneakers.

Boxer slowed. He had three choices: to run, to turn around, or to continue to move toward them. Whatever the choice, there wasn't any way to avoid a confrontation. If he ran, they'd be after him like a shot, and he'd much prefer to have them where he could see them. The same applied to turning around. That left him with only one viable option.

The three men blocked his way.

"You're making a mistake," Boxer said, hoping to bluff them before they took any action.

"No mistake, mister," the Black man said. "Just give us your watch, that ring you're wearing, and your wallet —"

Boxer's right leg shot out, and he landed a kick in the man's groin that doubled him up.

The other two went for their switchblades and with dangerous flicking motions began to circle Boxer.

"You're going to bleed," one of them said.

"Why don't you take your friend there," Boxer said, gesturing toward the man on the ground, "and leave while you can."

One of them stabbed at Boxer, who dodged the thrust.

"You're making a mistake," Boxer told them again. "A big mistake."

They continued to circle him.

Boxer suddenly reached around to the broad of his back, and the next moment, he pointed a snubnosed .38 at them. "It's loaded," he said calmly. Then, with much more authority, "Drop the knives."

The two men froze.

"Drop the knives," Boxer ordered.

They obeyed.

"Put your hands on your heads," Boxer told them. "Good. Now, when I count to three you run as fast as you can, because after I see you, I'll put a bullet in each of your legs. Understand?"

The two men nodded, and the taller one asked, "What about Juris?"

"Juris is still throwing up," Boxer said. "You can come back for him later."

"But —"

"I'm going to start counting, and you better start running," Boxer told them. A moment later, he said, "Now..." The two men sprinted off, before he started the count. He waited until they were out of sight, then bending down to Juris, he said, "If I were real mean, I'd crack this gun across your face a couple of times... Break your nose... Open your head in a few places."

Juris shrank away.

Then suddenly Boxer had an idea and asked, "What's your full name?"

"Juris Porter."

"Have you got a sheet?" Boxer asked.

"Nothin' serious."

"Give me an example."

"A couple of cars —"

"Armed robbery?" Boxer asked.

Juris dropped his eyes. "You a fuckin' mind reader?"

"I'm not a fucking anything" Boxer said. "But for you and your dumb friends this could turn out to be the luckiest night of your lives."

"What you talkin' 'bout? You want us to pull a job for you?"

"I want to *give* you a job," Boxer said. "A real job."

Juris squinted up at him.

"Tomorrow morning, at ten a.m. you and your two friends come to the Washington Hotel. I'll be in the lobby waiting for you. Ten a.m., not one minute later. You understand?"

Juris nodded. "What kind of job?"

"You'll find out tomorrow morning," Boxer said, reaching behind himself to put the revolver away.

"What's your name?" Juris asked.

Boxer reached down and helped Juris to his feet. "You'll find that out tomorrow morning. Remember, not a minute after ten."

"Yeah, I heard you," Juris said, and, rubbing his genitals, he added, "You kick like a fuckin' mule."

Boxer grinned. "I warned you and your friends that you were making a mistake."

Juris nodded. "You warned us, man," he answered.

"See you tomorrow morning," Boxer said, then he turned around and started to walk back to the hotel.

CHAPTER 9

By the time Boxer returned to his hotel room, he was tired and more depressed than when he'd left it. He switched on the TV and found nothing on any of the channels that held his interest. He spent a half-hour trying to call Stark, gave up, and decided to go to sleep.

It didn't take him long to undress, shower, and get into bed. He was just drifting off when the phone rang.

Kate was on the other end. He recognized her voice immediately.

"I can't sleep," she said. "Can you?"

"I was almost —"

"Don't tell me I woke you?"

"You did," he answered.

"I tried calling you earlier," she told him. "I thought we should settle this matter about the book."

"It's settled," Boxer answered.

"Not the way it should be," she replied.

"It's settled," he repeated.

"Can't we talk?" Kate asked.

"I don't have anything more to say. Besides, I'm tired. I had a long day."

"I'm a good listener."

"I don't like talking on the phone," Boxer said.

"To show you what a good sport I am, I'll come to your room," she told him.

He caught the hint of laughter in her voice. "Just where the hell are you?"

"Across the hall," she answered, now openly laughing.

Boxer laughed too.

"Just open your door, and I'll pop across the hall," Kate said.

"You don't miss a beat, do you?"

"Not when I want something," she responded, then asked, "Do we parley?"

"Whatever we do, it won't get me to change my mind," he said. "The risk is all yours."

"I'll take it," she said and clicked off.

Boxer left the bed, went to the door, and opened it. Kate was standing in the doorway of her room. The light coming from behind her passed through the white diaphanous peignoir set silhouetting every curve of her body.

She closed the door after her, crossed the hallway, and passing him, she entered the room, filling it with her floral-scented perfume.

"No promises," Boxer said.

"None asked," she answered in a throaty voice, opening the bowed ribbon that held the filmy robe closed.

Boxer went back to the bed and made room for her.

She slipped the robe off and let it drop to the floor. She removed the right shoulder strap of her nightgown, then the left. The gown slipped to the floor. Naked, she stood very still, and in a whisper, just loud enough for him to hear, she asked, "Do you like what you see?"

"Very much," he answered sotto voce.

Kate lay down next to him.

Boxer took her in his arms.

When it was over, neither of them spoke. He held her in his arms and they slept. Boxer awoke at first light.

Kate was nestled against him. The perfume she wore still clung to her. She was really a lovely-looking woman.

"How long have you been looking at me?" Kate asked.

"Not long."

She glanced at the window, then at him. "It's gray out there."

"The sun hasn't come up yet... Why don't we go back to sleep," he suggested. Looking at her naked made him want her again.

"Is that your way of telling me to go?"

He put his tanned arm around her bare stomach.

"If I wanted you to go, then I would have told you to go."

Kate took a deep breath and relaxed against him.

"I'm going to be leaving this afternoon," Boxer said. "I have to spend some time with a friend, but I should be back in a couple of days."

"I'll call you," she said.

"In a month or so, I'll be gone for six weeks, maybe longer," he said, thinking about the salvage operation.

"Where?"

"He put his finger across her lips. "If we're going to have a relationship, the one thing you must accept is my silence about what I do and where I go."

She put his finger in her mouth and sucked on it. "I'm a professional journalist —"

"Not when you are with me," he said. "When you're with me you're just a woman who wants me to make love to her, and I'm just a man who wants to make love to her."

"Now?" she asked.

"Yes, now," Boxer said...

The ringing of the phone woke Boxer.

Kate too was startled into wakefulness by the sound.

Boxer picked up the phone and said, "Boxer here."

Admiral Pierce was on the other end. "You have a go on that project," he said.

"Without any exceptions?"

"A total go," Pierce answered.

"Good."

"There is one detail I should mention," Pierce said.

Boxer had pulled himself up and was now leaning against the back of the bed. Kate rested her head against his chest. "Give me the one detail," he said.

"Because of our present political involvement with the Soviets — *glasnost* — we thought it best to include them in the salvage operation. I even suggested to my counterpart in Moscow that Admiral Borodine head their team."

Boxer was about to become angry, but suddenly he realized that the Russians did have a legitimate reason for being there, since the gold had been theirs originally.

"Admiral Borodine is here in Washington, as you well know, and since the two of you have worked together on other projects, there won't be any time wasted for each of you to adjust to the other."

"Good thinking," Admiral Boxer said.

"When will you be ready to start?" Pierce asked.

"By the beginning of next week."

"Excellent!" Pierce responded.

"I'll be in touch, sir," Boxer said, then he put the phone down.

"Business?" Kate asked, tilting her face up toward his and at the same time running the balls of her fingers over his chest.

Boxer nodded, then glancing at his chronographic watch, he said, "It's almost nine, and I have a ten o'clock appointment."

"Anyone I should know?" she asked casually.

Boxer eased her away from him. "If you want to meet three muggers, you're welcome to come with me," he told her on the way to the bathroom.

"What?" she cried, sitting back on her heels. "Muggers?"

Boxer ran the water for his shave. "I ran into them last night," he called out.

She left the bed and stood naked just outside the open bathroom door. "You didn't tell me that."

"I didn't tell you a lot of things," he answered, scraping the lather from his face with a barber's razor.

"Good lord, I didn't think anyone used that kind of razor anymore."

Boxer laughed and said, "You see, there are lots of things you don't know."

"Tell me about the muggers," she pressed. "Did they try to take you?"

Boxer rinsed the soap off of the blade, dried it, and then turned on the shower.

"Well, did they?" Kate questioned.

"What they tried is history. Soon they'll have a chance for the future," Boxer said, and he stepped into the shower, closing the door behind.

"You are an infuriating man!" Kate exclaimed.

"Good," Boxer answered above the sound of the shower, then he added, "If you want to meet them, better get dressed, although I'm sure that they wouldn't mind looking at you just the way you are."

"Funny," she yelled back at him.

"I'll meet you down in the lobby," Boxer told her. "If I'm not there, I'll be in the hotel coffee shop."

"I wouldn't miss this meeting for the world," Kate called out.

Boxer continued to shower, knowing that Kate had returned to her own room. Shortly, he shut the water off, stepped out of the shower, and began to dry himself.

A few minutes later he was dressed. He wore black slacks, a light blue sport shirt, and a houndstooth jacket. He reached the lobby at five to ten, and the three black-leather-jacketed men were waiting off to one side. They looked more ill at ease than small boys waiting their turn in a dentist's office. And the people who glanced at them appeared to be equally uncomfortable.

Boxer went straight toward them. They seemed almost relieved to see him. What was that old adage? Something about a friendly face — He wasn't exactly their friend, but he was someone they knew, or at least had previous dealings with… Some dealings!

"Well, we here," Juris Porter said.

"You guys have breakfast yet?" Boxer asked.

"Coffee and a couple of doughnuts," the taller of the other men said.

"Breakfast," Boxer said. "It's on my tab."

The four of them trooped into the coffee shop, where several hotel guests and local office types were breakfasting. Boxer pointed to a booth. "We'll need a chair," he said. "A lady is going to join us."

"No damn guidance woman, I hope," Juris said. "I be sick of those."

His friends agreed and emphasized their agreement by slapping each others' palms.

Boxer ignored him and said, "Listen, when you're with me, you cut the shit stuff out."

The three young men looked at each other, then Juris said, "Hey, bro, what'd you bring us here for?"

"Good question. First, I want the names of your friends," Boxer said. "If you're going to work for me, I should know your name."

The taller man leaned forward. "You want us to pull —"

"I said 'work,'" Boxer told him. "Now give me your name."

"Alex Crespo."

"And yours?" Boxer asked, looking straight at the shortest in the trio.

"Pepe Zapeda," the young man answered.

Boxer nodded and said, "I'm Admiral Jack Boxer."

"Hey, aren't you the guy that just got rescued?" Alex asked.

Boxer nodded.

Juris whooped, "Man, man, if that ain't somethin'! Guys, I got put down by a fuckin' admiral."

He was loud enough to be heard throughout the coffee shop and drew everyone's attention to the table.

Boxer managed a smile.

The waitress came over and asked if they were ready to order.

"Sausages and eggs, the eggs over well," Boxer said. "One slice of rye toast, grapefruit juice, and coffee."

"I'll have the same," Juris told the waitress.

Alex said, "Yeah, that sounds good."

Pepe added, "Me too."

When the waitress left the table, Boxer said, "In a few days I will need a couple of dozen men to work on a salvage operation."

"You mean, like in the water?" Alex asked.

"Deep in the water. But you will not be involved in any of the underwater work. I'll need you on deck."

"How much are you willing to pay?"

"Five hundred a week, starting from the moment you board the salvage vessel," Boxer said.

"Sounds good," Juris said.

"Where is the work goin' to be done?" Pepe asked.

"At sea, several thousands of miles from here."

"What will we do?" Juris asked.

"Whatever you're told to do," Boxer answered. "Once you sign on, you also sign to accept the ship's rules."

"How long will the job last?" Crespo asked.

Boxer shrugged. "It could be over in a matter of days, if we're lucky, or it could last several months. It all depends on what the divers find when they make their investigatory dives."

"Holy shit, I haven't had straight job for over a year," Crespo said.

"Yeah, that's about it for me too," Pepe said.

Boxer nodded and was about to seal the arrangement with a handshake, when suddenly he realized that Crespo and Alex, who were sitting opposite him, were bug-eyed. He looked over his shoulder toward the door. Kate was coming toward them. She wore a black leather miniskirt; a yellow blouse, open to the third button; and black leather vest. Everyone was gawking at her: the men with open lust, and the women flaming envy.

Boxer stood up.

She came straight to him, put her hands on his shoulders, and before he could say anything, she kissed him on the mouth.

"Man, that's what I call a goo-oo-d mornin' kiss," Pepe commented.

Despite the fire in his cheeks, Boxer said, "Juris, will you get a chair for Ms. Brennan?"

"Sure thing, Jack — I mean, Admiral," Juris answered, sliding out of the booth.

In the few moments that it took Juris to return with a chair, Boxer introduced the other two young men. Then when Juris returned, he introduced him.

"It's a pleasure to meet you," Kate said, flashing them a very bright smile.

"She goin' with us?" Alex asked.

Boxer shook his head. The color flashed in his cheeks again. He hadn't had time to warm them to keep silent about the salvage operation.

"No, but I'd like to," she said.

"What about it, Admiral?" Pepe asked.

"I'm afraid not," Boxer answered.

"An' I thought admirals could do —"

"Drop it," Boxer snapped.

The three men checked one another, then Juris said, "Okay, you say 'drop it,' an' it's dropped."

The waitress returned to the table and asked if Kate wanted anything.

"Just orange juice, coffee, and a toasted bagel with butter on the side," she answered. Then turning her attention back to Boxer, she said, "Don't let me interrupt anything."

"You already have," he answered, aware that she was rubbing her leg against his.

"Are these the three that tried to mug you last night?" she asked, now scanning the young men at the table.

"It wasn't a real try," Boxer answered. "They were just having some fun. Isn't that right?"

"Practicin' for the real thing," Crespo said.

The waitress served the four orders of sausages and eggs and told Kate, "Yours will be out in a couple of minutes."

"No hurry," Kate answered, then smiling at Boxer, she added, "I'm enjoying myself so much that I'll be sorry when I have to leave." She continued to play footsy with Boxer, even as she spoke to the waitress.

Boxer said, "After breakfast, I'm going to rent a car and drive down the coast a ways to see my friend. Do you guys want a lift?"

"We got nothin' special goin'" Juris responded.

Boxer thought for a moment, then said, "If you feel like taking a ride, why don't the three of you come with me. It will give you a chance to meet Admiral Stark."

"Is he goin' to be with us too?" Alex questioned.

"Yes," Boxer said with a nod.

"Does that mean you'll be back here tonight?" Kate asked, looking at Boxer.

"Late."

Smiling conspiratorially, she said, "We still have so much to talk about."

Boxer permitted that statement to slide by. He'd hoped that she understood his position on the subject of his biography. But he also recognized that she was a persistent woman, and he'd experienced a sufficient number of that sisterhood to realize that she was an elite member.

By eleven o'clock, Boxer and his entourage were walking out of the coffee shop.

"Well, thank you for breakfast, Jack," Kate said. "And it was a pleasure to meet you gentlemen."

The three young men stammered, almost in unison, "Yeah, it be great... Man, really great!"

Boxer concealed a smile.

"We'll talk," Kate said, throwing her arms around Boxer's neck and kissing him on the mouth again.

Luk Shen Koo Gul sat at his desk in New York's Chinatown, smoked a three-dollar cigar, and looked down on the Bowery through a window that hadn't been washed for as long as he could remember. It was one of those freaky days that sometimes came to New York in the middle of February, which really belonged to late April or early May, where everyone took off their coats, jackets, and sweaters. It gave him great pleasure to look at all the young women who passed beneath the window. Despite the fact that he was one of the biggest whoremasters in the neighborhood, he had a weakness for beautiful women, gambling of any sort, and ran a gun-for-hire operation equal to any in San Francisco or, for that matter, even Hong Kong.

Luk Shen Koo Gul had just caught sight of a lovely nubile woman of eighteen or nineteen, and as he began to puff rapidly on his cigar, the phone rang.

The second time it rang, he gave it a quick, dirty look — "Shit!" he exploded, taking the cigar out of his mouth. He glared at the phone, which now was ringing a third time, and picking it up, he barked, "No fuckin' here!" Then, he slammed it back into its cradle.

He started for the door, but before he reached it, the phone started to ring again. This time, he spoke Cantonese when he answered it.

The voice on the other end said, "This is Fong Shun Un, Uncle."

Fong Shun Un wasn't really his nephew. They weren't related by blood or by marriage. Fong Shun Un's mother had been his mistress before she married that crazy German, Mittenkope.

"Uncle, are you still there?" Fong Shun Un called.

"Yes, yes... I was just thinking about your dear mother. How is she?"

"Well, thank you, Uncle," Fong Shun Un answered. "She sends her best to you."

"Send her my best too." Then he said, "I read that your father was rescued, along with several others."

"Uncle, that's why I'm calling you," Fong Shun Un said.

"Oh!"

"He and his friends must be found."

"Why?" Luk Shen Koo Gul asked as he dropped into the chair behind the desk and put his feet on the top of it.

Fong Shun Un told him about the charts.

"Very interesting," Luk Shen Koo Gul commented. "I am more than willing to help you, Nephew. But I cannot take risks without adequate compensation."

"How adequate would the compensation have to be in order for you to take the risk?" Fong Shun Un asked.

"I am not a greedy man," Luk Shen Koo Gul replied. "I live modestly, so ten million U.S. dollars should be adequate."

"That is no problem."

"Better make it fifteen," Luk Shen Koo Gul said, "That should make me happy."

"Uncle, I want you to be happy," Fong Shun Un said.

"Good. We have a deal."

"We have a deal," Fong Shun Un echoed, then he added, "Should anyone try to stop you from taking the charts, kill —"

"Nephew, it is bad luck to speak of death after closing a deal," Luk Shen Koo Gul reminded him.

"I am humbly sorry," Fong Shun Un responded.

"Besides, I know my business," Luk Shen Koo Gul said.

"Certainly, Uncle," Fong Shun Un answered, instantly realizing that he'd said the wrong thing.

"When will you be in New York?" Luk Shen asked.

"Two days. My brother will be with me."

"You will be my guests," the mobster said. "Call from the airport before you leave. By the way, where are you?"

"Hong Kong."

"A wonderful place for food and women."

"Yes, it is."

"So remember to call before you leave. You will be met by one of my men at the airport."

"Thank you, Uncle. My brother and I are honored," Fong Shun Un responded in the most respectful voice he could muster.

Luk Shen Koo Gul put the phone down and puffed his cigar back to life.

CHAPTER 10

Boxer and Stark walked along the beach, leaving Mittenkope, Juris, Pepe, and Alex back at the house. Both men were silent. Boxer smoked his pipe and Stark, his cigar. They had spent a couple of hours talking about the salvage operation, and now each was content to be left alone with his thoughts.

Boxer wasn't doing any thinking, but he did appreciate the silence between them. It permitted him to concentrate on the sound of the breaking surf, the high-pitched cries of the seagulls, and the play of light that resulted from the movements of the clouds across the face of the sun.

"What time do you plan on leaving?" Stark asked, finally breaking the silence.

"I figured all of us would go down to the Chowder House for dinner," Boxer answered. "I planned to be back in D.C. about eleven-thirty, midnight at the very latest."

"Sounds good to me," Stark said. Then, with a smile, "I see you're in the Good Samaritan business again. Those three hooligans should probably be serving time."

"Probably," Boxer answered.

"You think you can trust them to do an honest day's work? You know it won't be easy on the ship, and if they give us trouble — well, there's not a hell of a lot you can do about it."

Boxer puffed on his pipe before he said, "I don't know if I can trust them, and as far as doing an honest day's work, I'd be damned surprised if in their entire lives they ever worked at a job for a full day." Then he stopped walking and took the pipe out of his mouth. "I'm not offering them charity: I'm offering them a chance to become human beings."

Stark didn't answer.

Automatically they turned back toward the house to return.

Boxer said nothing about Chuck, his adopted son, who had gone down aboard the submarine *Manta*, three years before, but he had taken Chuck off the streets too, and the boy became a naval officer. Maybe he was taking the three hooligans, as Stark had rightly called them, off the streets because he knew that Chuck would have appreciated the gesture. Thoughts about Chuck immediately brought forth memories about his girlfriend, Francine... He uttered a ragged sigh.

"Anything wrong, Jack?" Stark asked.

Boxer shook his head and puffed hard on his pipe.

They were approximately halfway to the house when Stark suddenly stopped and said, "I have something I want to say to you."

"Oh?"

"I've never become involved in your personal life, have I?" Stark asked.

"Never," Boxer answered.

"Okay, but this time, I'm going to," Stark told him.

"Sounds serious."

Stark nodded. "I've watched you for awhile now, and I don't like what I see."

"Sorry, I can't change what I look like," Boxer answered flippantly.

"But you can change the way you act," Stark said. "Just listen to me. I don't want to discuss anything... I want you to listen, and then think about what I said."

Boxer nodded. Stark seldom took the father role, even though in many, many respects, over the years of their association, the man had become his surrogate father. Stark had made him his legal heir.

"You take chances that you shouldn't, you're depressed most of the time, and when you're not, you're absolutely manic. You haven't put either Chuck or Francine behind you. I thought the cruise would be the answer, and maybe even Louise... But when the two of you said goodbye in Hong Kong, that was that, as far as you were concerned."

Boxer nodded, but said nothing.

"Jack, if you don't find a woman —"

"Admiral —"

"No, listen to me. I never married, but I wish I had. It's no great thing to be alone, Jack. No great thing. And that's where you're heading."

"I've thought about it," Boxer said.

"Then, for God's sake do something about it, Jack, before you're too old to really meld with a woman, before you become too old to change your ways. That's what happened to me. Then, one day I woke up, and there I was a crotchety old man."

"You? Never," Boxer said, trying to lighten the mood a bit. "You're not crotchety; you're just cantankerous."

Stark glowered at him.

"All right, I promise to think about what you have said," Boxer told him.

Stark's expression changed to one of doubt.

"Really, I will," Boxer assured him. "I promise."

"I hope you do," Stark said, and he started to walk again.

Boxer picked up the step and said, "Suddenly, I've become very hungry."

"I suddenly feel that way too," Stark responded.

"Must be all this advice of yours about my finding a wife," Boxer said in a nonchalant voice. "Maybe we became hungry in anticipation of all the good cooking she might do."

"Don't be a wise guy!"

"By God, you're right, Admiral; you are crotchety. And here I accused you of being cantankerous," Boxer said straight-faced.

Stark shook his head. "Naturally, I know that you'll do precisely what you want to do."

"Precisely," Boxer answered.

They looked at one another and exploded into laughter.

It was a quarter to twelve when Boxer went to the hotel desk and asked the clerk if there were any messages for him.

"Admiral Borodine called," the clerk said, handing the pink message slip to him.

Boxer thanked him and glanced at the piece of paper. "Call anytime up to oh-one-hundred," the message read, and it gave his home number.

Boxer rode the elevator up to his floor. As he unlocked and entered his room, about to switch on the lights, a woman's voice said, "Don't do that."

"Kate?" he asked, though he was certain it was her.

"I hope you weren't expecting anyone else," she answered.

"I wasn't expecting you," he said, closing the door. "I have to make an important phone call."

"Here, this should help," Kate said, switching on the lamp on the end table next to the bed. She was naked.

Boxer went directly to the phone and dialed Borodine's number.

"Jack?" Borodine asked.

"Yes."

"I've been assigned to the salvage operation," Borodine said.

"I hoped you would be," Boxer said.

"We'll have four divers, myself, and a dozen technicians, and one medical doctor, a woman named Ilia Ioff."

"Good," Boxer said, then he asked about Borodine's wife and child.

"Doing fine," Borodine said. "Tanya wants you to come to dinner on Friday night. Can you make it?"

"I'll be there," Boxer said.

"Bring someone with you, if you want," Borodine said. "I know Ilia will be there. It turns out she's an old friend of Tanya's."

"I will bring a friend," Boxer said, looking at Kate, who was now seductively stretched out on the bed, smiling at him.

"Make it nineteen-thirty," Borodine said, then added, "Good night, Jack."

"Good night, Igor," Boxer responded and put the phone down.

"So you're going to take me to meet your Russian friend," Kate commented with obvious pleasure, as she went through the motions of a catlike stretch, then turning over on her stomach.

Boxer went to the bed and looked down at Kate. There wasn't any doubt about it — from any perspective, she was well put together. "You're damn sure of yourself, aren't you?"

She swiveled her head to one side, and, looking up at him, she told him, "Only now and then."

"And I'm a *now*?" he asked.

"Far from it. If anyone is the *now*, I am," she replied.

Boxer slapped her on the butt.

"Hey, that wasn't called for," she complained. "Not too many single men come back to their hotel room, and find a woman waiting for them."

"It has happened once or twice before you came up with the bright idea," Boxer said, starting to undress.

Kate turned sideways and rested on her chin in the palm of her hand. "What in God's name were you doing with those three creatures today?"

"They're going to work for me."

"Scaring little old ladies and children?"

"Don't be funny." He was about to say something else when he heard the doorknob slowly being tried. He pointed to the door, then crossed his lips with a finger. A moment later, he had the .38 in his hand, and after he fitted a silencer to the muzzle, he switched off the lamp.

"What the hell is going on?" Kate whispered.

"Get down on the floor, on the other side of the bed," he told her, ignoring her question. "Move now!"

Boxer crawled to the door, stood up, and positioned himself to its left side.

The person on the other side of the door used a plastic card to open the lock and began to slowly turn the knob.

Boxer's heart raced. He could hear the blood pound in his ears.

The door began to swing open, inch by inch.

The light from the hallway spilled onto the floor of the room and with it came a slowly lengthening shadow.

Boxer sucked in his breath.

A .357 with a silencer on the muzzle came through the opening.

Boxer leveled the .38 at the hand holding the .357, and as he exhaled, he squeezed the trigger.

The man screamed and dropped the .357.

Boxer pushed back the door, but the man ran and was already at the exit to the stairwell.

"He came here to kill you!" Kate exclaimed, lifting herself off the floor.

Boxer picked up the revolver and closed the door. He had only managed to get a quick glance at the man, but it was long enough for him to see that he was Chinese.

"If you hadn't been here —"

Boxer cut her short. "I was, and it might stop you from climbing into a man's bed when he's not there." He put both guns down on the desk.

"Aren't you going to do anything?" she asked, getting on the bed and sitting back on her heels.

"Shower, then get into bed," Boxer said. He knew that if he called the police, the detectives would only go through the motions of an investigation. Tomorrow, he'd notify the Company and Pierce. Their people would be much more effective on something like this, than civil authorities.

"I might leave while you're showering."

"You might, then again you might not," Boxer answered. "I won't know until I come out, will I?"

"Now who's being sure of himself?" Kate asked.

"A man who realizes that something can go either way can't exactly be accused of being sure of himself," Boxer said, unzipping his pants.

Kate didn't answer.

Boxer stripped off his skivvies and walked into the bathroom. As he closed the door, he called out, "Try to keep out of trouble for the next few minutes."

"You're... You're —"

Boxer didn't wait to hear what he was. He closed the door.

"I could fall in love with you," Kate said, her voice almost a whisper.

Several minutes before they had climaxed, and now were enjoying the afterglow that came from being sexually sated.

"Do you think you could fall in love with me?" she asked.

"Not if you continue to ask all sorts of questions," Boxer answered.

"Can't you ever give a decent answer?" she questioned, her voice at least an octave above its normal tone.

"I don't fall in and out of love that easily. I enjoy making love to a woman, and I enjoy having a woman making love to me. And yes, enjoying being with the person. But — and it's a big *but* — that has very little to do with really loving someone. Notice, Kate, I didn't say anything about *being in love*; I said *loving someone*."

"Haven't you ever loved someone?" Kate asked.

"Yes."

"And?"

"Things change," Boxer said softly.

Their conversation lapsed.

"Do you want to make love again?" Kate asked.

"No," he answered.

"You know, I'm really a very nice person," Kate said.

"I never thought that you weren't. Eager, even pushy, when it came to your work, but that's what a good reporter needs to be."

"I'm not just a reporter," she said. "I'm a writer, an author, or at least that's what I want to be; and I will. I just need that one break, that one book —"

Boxer removed his hand from her body and put it on his chest. "Much of what I have done is still top secret," he said.

"But I really don't know what is still in that category and what has been declassified."

"If anything has been declassified, would you tell me about it?" she asked.

Boxer uttered a deep sigh. He actually felt that he owed her something. "I'll try —"

"You will!" she cried suddenly, bolting into a sitting position. "You really will?"

"I'll try, but I can't promise that I'll be a good storyteller."

"That's my job," she said proudly. "Oh, I know I can do it. I know it!"

Boxer laughed at her childlike enthusiasm.

"You don't think —"

"I think you can, and probably will, but now let's go to sleep. In just a few hours, I have to attend a meeting."

She settled down next to him.

"By the way, how did you manage to get in here?" Boxer questioned.

"Shouldn't you have asked that question some time ago?"

"I would have, but each time I was going to, something else came up."

"You mean you let a little thing like a man who came to kill you stop you?" Kate teased.

"Let's say it diverted my attention," Boxer replied.

"And of course making love to me also diverted your attention?"

"Absolutely," Boxer responded.

For several moments, neither of them spoke.

"Hold me," Kate said.

"Now how am I supposed to sleep?" Boxer asked.

"That's your problem. Good night, Jack."

"Good night," he answered.

Luk Shen Koo Gul paced back and forth in the living room of his apartment, which was located in a four-floor walk-up on Mott Street.

Hok Chen stood in the center of the room, which was elaborately decorated with Chinese paintings, and heavy Victorian furniture.

"I send you to do a job, and you get shot at," Luk Shen Koo Gul said, speaking in Chinese.

"He was waiting for me," Hok Chen mumbled.

"How —"

"He was... I opened the door, and the next thing I heard was a pop, and the gun was torn out of my hand. My goddamn wrist hurts like hell."

Luk Shen Koo Gul made a face.

"There was a woman in the room too," Hok Chen said.

"How do you know that?"

"Perfume, there was the smell of perfume in the room."

"Woman, eh? Interesting, very interesting," Luk Shen Koo Gul commented. "Maybe we get the woman and exchange her for the charts."

"Maybe... But don't you think we should first find out who she is?" Hok Chen said.

"You do it. Go get some sleep, then go back to the hotel and find out," Luk Shen said.

"Then what?"

"Bring her to Madame Shahad Khun."

"You want her in the whorehouse?"

"Best place for her. If we don't get charts, she works, just like all the girls. Nobody gets a free ride," Luk Shen Koo Gul said. "Nobody!"

CHAPTER 11

Kahn said, "Originally, I thought you'd be working off the sister ship to the Explorer *Glomare*, the Explorer *Terra*, but now I have had other thoughts."

Boxer braced himself. Experience had taught him that whenever Kahn said he had other thoughts they were generally bad.

"Are you listening?" Kahn asked.

"With both ears."

"We've modified a Franklin-type submarine for deep-water salvage, and this would be a good chance to test it. She carries two manned submersibles, two unmanned, and can carry a third on her deck."

"What's her operating depth?" Boxer asked.

"Modified, four thousand feet," Kahn replied.

"How was she modified, aside from the installation of high-tech gear?"

"Do you recall the use of the viscous —"

"Yes," Boxer said, remembering how one of his commands had been fitted with a viscous plastic that hardened under high pressure and returned to its normal consistency at atmospheric pressure.

"This boat has been fitted with a thin ceramic-like shell whose hardness increases by a factor five for every thousand feet."

"Interesting."

The phone on Kahn's desk rang. He answered it, listened, and then said, "Send them in."

Boxer turned his head toward the door, and when it opened, he saw Pierce and Borodine enter.

"Hello, comrade," Borodine said, striding toward Boxer with his hand outstretched.

Boxer was on his feet immediately, shook Borodine's hand, then the two embraced and pounded one another on the back.

"I didn't expect to see you here today," Boxer said.

"I invited him this morning," Pierce said. "I thought it best that he be in on everything from the ground floor."

Boxer nodded.

"Gentlemen, we might as well move to a more comfortable setting," Kahn said, gesturing toward the far side of the room where there was a coffee table and several easy chairs. "I'll join you after I arrange to have coffee and some pastry brought in."

Boxer winked at Borodine, and as they began to walk to the chairs, he said in a voice loud enough for Kahn to hear, "He either got more money in his yearly budget, or he's anticipating our haul."

"Must you always rile him?" Pierce asked.

"It's kind of a ritual," Boxer answered.

"Neither," Kahn called out. "I just thought it would be nice to have coffee and some pastry."

"He's doing it to show he's human," Boxer said as he dropped into one of the dark brown leather chairs.

"Do you have the same kind of running battle with the head of the KGB?" Pierce questioned as he looked at the Russian admiral.

Borodine was a chunky man with piercing, cool blue eyes that at the moment were lit with laughter. "Let me say — unofficially, of course —"

"Certainly, unofficially," Boxer said, knowing full well what his friend's relationship was to Kahn's counterpart.

"If I were in a social situation where I could choose my company, I would not choose him," Borodine said.

"I think you, Comrade Admiral, and Admiral Boxer, must have been born either under the same star or perhaps have the same genetic coding," Pierce said.

"Neither. We just know good from bad," Boxer told him. "It's as simple as that."

"What's 'as simple as that'?" Kahn asked as he came up to join them.

Pierce hurriedly said, "Boxer was saying that the refitted Franklin was simple."

Kahn gave him a questioning look, but did not pursue the statement. Instead, he repeated his explanation of the Franklin's ceramic shell for Borodine's benefit.

"I assume the shell is outside the boat," Borodine said.

"It is," Kahn answered.

"And it is absolutely uniform?" Boxer questioned.

"To the best of my knowledge it is."

"We will have two submersibles aboard and can carry one more on the boat's deck," Boxer said, looking at Igor.

"We will supply the third," Borodine answered. "We will modify it to fit over your hatch. I assume that would be under it?"

"I am not sure," Kahn said.

"Our men could enter it from the deck, but that would entail using an airlock and waste time," Borodine said.

"If there isn't a hatch we could make one," Boxer told him.

"But that would alter the integrity of the ceramic coating," Kahn complained.

"I don't see that as a real problem," Pierce said. "We'll be diving in a maximum of eight hundred feet of water. After the salvage operation is completed, if it's necessary, the ceramic coating that had been removed to make way for the hatch could be patched back on."

"The matter could be settled right here and now, if we could get the deck plans for the boat," Boxer said.

"I'll get them," Kahn said, leaving his chair and going to the desk, where he picked up the phone.

"What about weapons?" Boxer asked.

"Four laser-guided torpedoes in the forward torpedo room, eight high-velocity Sea Darts. And one of the submersibles is armed with eight more of them."

"Should be enough," Borodine said.

"Should be, but might not be if Mittenkope's sons come after us."

"Mittenkope?" Borodine questioned.

Before Boxer could answer, a knock at the door brought a firm, "Come in," from Kahn.

A young man arrived with a tray carrying two thermo-carafes of coffee, four settings, pastry, and small pitchers of milk and cream. He had hardly set the tray down on the coffee table, when another knock at the door brought another snapped, "Come in," from Kahn. This time a young woman entered with the deck plans of the Franklin.

The boat, according to the plans, had a small escape hatch twenty feet forward of its retractable sail. With that question settled, Borodine again asked about Mittenkope.

Boxer explained who the man was, and his connection to the salvage operation.

"The name, when I heard it, sounded familiar," Borodine said, then he added, "I'm not sure that my government will approve of his participation."

"Explain that he has the charts," Boxer said, after he swallowed a piece of cheese pastry.

"Explain too, that we — that is, the United States — will salvage the gold with, or without, their participation."

"There's another way," Boxer suggested. "Never mention it at all. After all, he's just another member of the salvage team. You're not going to give any sort of report on the entire crew, are you?"

Borodine shook his head. "I won't, but you can be sure that one member of my team will be KGB, and he will — that is part of his job."

"We'll worry about that when it happens, Igor," Boxer answered. "Mittenkope won't bother anyone, I promise you that. It's his sons we have to worry about. I've already encountered someone whom they sent to kill me."

"What?" Kahn exploded, leaping out of his chair and spilling coffee on the table. "Why didn't you tell me?"

"I just did," Boxer answered.

"I mean earlier," Kahn responded, using a napkin to wipe up the spilled coffee.

"There was no hurry. I wanted to wait for the appropriate moment. It was bound to come up."

"What happened?" Pierce asked.

Boxer ran through the incident, but did not mention that Kate was with him. That part, as the official comment went on secret information, they did not have "the need to know."

"You hit him?" Kahn asked.

"His gun only. I imagine the man has a very sore wrist," Boxer said.

"And you think he's Chinese?"

"I'm almost certain."

"I'll have my people check it out," Kahn said.

"ONI will get on it too," Pierce said. "But in the meantime, it wouldn't hurt for you to have a couple of heavies guard you."

Boxer shook his head. "The only thing I want is a 9mm automatic."

"That's no problem. You'll have one before you leave Langley this morning," Kahn told him.

"How much trouble do you think Mittenkope's two sons will give us, once we're at sea?" Borodine asked.

"My guess is that they'll do everything they can to get their hands on the gold," Boxer said.

"Are you sure they know about it?"

"Yes. Mittenkope told them about it, but never permitted them to see the charts. At least, that's what he told me, and I have no reason to disbelieve him."

"How long will it take for you to assemble a crew?" Kahn asked.

"Not more than ten days," Boxer answered, then, looking at Pierce, he added, "I want Paskudnyak assigned to the operation."

Pierce and Kahn exchanged glances.

"Let me put it this way —" Boxer began.

"You don't have to put it any way; you have him," Pierce said.

Boxer nodded appreciatively.

"Those ten will give us time to familiarize ourselves with the boat. Then, when the entire complement is assembled, we will make a quick shakedown and a deep-water dive off the Chesapeake."

"How long will all of that take?" Kahn asked.

"What do you think, Igor, five days?" Boxer asked.

"Yes, five days should do it," Borodine answered.

Kahn checked the calendar on his desk. "Then you should be on your way the twenty-fifth of this month," he said.

"That's about right."

"And the actual salvage operation should begin — say, three to four days after that."

"More like a week," Boxer answered. "It will take us three days to reach the wreck and several more before we finish reconnoitering her. Remember, we don't know how she's positioned, and we must get into her main storage area."

Kahn nodded.

"From what I understand, you don't want to spend too much time there this time of the year."

"We'll try to make it quick and clean," Boxer said. "But there are always problems, and there's no way of anticipating what they will be."

"Do you want a surface ship on station with you?" Pierce asked.

"I think it would be a good idea," Borodine said. "It would give us a greater margin of safety."

Boxer agreed.

"It should not be a Navy vessel," Borodine commented. "An oceangoing tug would be fine. It should be large enough to carry decompression chambers, should we need them, and other kinds of emergency equipment."

"A chopper might be a good thing to have," Boxer said.

"We have an oceangoing yacht that has a chopper pad built over the stern, and it can handle the kind of emergency gear you might need," Kahn said.

"We'll go with it, but only if it's manned by Navy personnel. I don't want any Company men around to muck up things."

Kahn's face turned red. "That was uncalled for," he said.

"It was called for. I don't want to have to deal with a problem that, in the first place, shouldn't have come up. Wherever your people are, there's a problem."

"You're one of my people," Kahn said.

"Only on the books," Boxer answered.

"All right. Boxer, let's get on with this," Pierce said. "You'll have Navy people where you want them."

Boxer nodded and asked where the boat was located.

"Norfolk," Kahn answered.

"Cut my orders, and I'll go down to take command on Monday," Boxer said.

"They'll be delivered to you at the hotel," Pierce said.

"I guess that about wraps it up," Boxer commented.

"It does," Kahn answered testily.

After Boxer, Borodine, and Pierce left Kahn's office, Pierce explained that he had another meeting to go to and hurried away.

"Well, I'm free for this afternoon anyway," Boxer commented to Borodine as they walked out of the building and into the parking area.

"It's a beautiful fall day," Borodine said.

"Everything still on for dinner Friday night?" Boxer asked.

"Certainly. Tanya is looking forward to seeing you," Borodine said.

"And how's your boy?" Boxer questioned.

"Growing faster than a weed," Borodine replied. "He asks about you all the time. He wants to know how I met you."

Boxer laughed. "And what do you answer?"

"That we met under very peculiar circumstances," Borodine said.

"That hardly describes two men who were determined to kill each other."

"He's too young to understand that," Borodine said. Then in a wistful voice, he added, "I really hope and pray that he never has to understand it."

"You're right there," Boxer agreed.

They reached Borodine's car first, and he said, "This woman that you will meet at dinner is a very special lady."

Boxer smiled knowingly and wagged his finger at Borodine.

"No, it's nothing like that," Borodine quickly answered. "Her husband —"

"And here I thought you were trying to make a match between —"

"Her husband is dead," Borodine said. "He was a cosmonaut… His spaceship exploded on reentry. That was three years ago."

"Was that the accident over the Arctic?"

Borodine nodded. "He tried to make an emergency landing in Siberia, near the Bering Strait."

Boxer said nothing. He knew several women who had lost their husbands, and no two reacted the same way. Some managed to live with the loss and build a new life for themselves, while others, either out of guilt or remorse, fell apart. He was waiting for Borodine to tell him on which side of the fence Dr. Ioff wound up.

"She's just coming out of her shell," Borodine said. "I have an idea that the marriage wasn't all that good, and when Gregory — that was her husband's name — was killed, it provided her with the freedom she'd wanted. But at a price."

"Guilt?"

"A million metric tons of it," Borodine answered.

"Is that why she's part of your team?" Boxer asked, immediately concerned that she might not be fit to spend a long period underwater, or more importantly, keep a cool head during an emergency

"No. She's a good doctor, by Soviet standards, and since we needed one, she was my first choice. She is presently a staff physician at the Moscow State Hospital but is here as part of an exchange program with the Naval Hospital at Bethesda, Maryland. She is on her way to becoming a specialist in internal medicine."

"But why tell me all of this?" Boxer asked.

"Because she knows who you are."

"What? How could she?"

Borodine smiled.

"Am I supposed to understand what that grin means?"

"She's my sister," Borodine answered.

"Sister? When the hell did you acquire a sister? You're an only child — well, aren't you?"

"It was a second marriage for my father. She's his child, but she was adopted and raised by her stepfather, who, by the way, was also a medical doctor."

"I thought you said she was Tanya's friend," Boxer said.

"She is. The two of them became very good friends. Tanya knew her long before she knew me."

Boxer ran his hand across his chin. "This is too damn weird for me to comment on," he said.

Borodine laughed. "I had a feeling you'd say something like that."

"All right, I guess if I could live with you, I could manage to do the same with her," Boxer responded.

"Jack, you make it seem as if I'm a difficult person to get along with... Hell, after we stopped trying to kill each other, I actually got to like you," Borodine said, grinning at him.

"Yeah, the first hurdle is always the toughest," Boxer responded with a straight face.

"See you Friday night," Borodine said, highballing him.

Boxer returned the salute. "See you," he said as he turned to open his car, and Borodine walked away.

By late afternoon, the sky had turned from teal blue to gray, promising rain, and the wind had shifted to the northeast, bringing with it the damp chill of the North Atlantic.

Boxer returned to his hotel, checked the desk for messages. Stark had been the only caller.

On the way up to his room, Boxer suddenly realized that his mood had shifted. It was now as gray as the weather. And by the time the elevator stopped and he stepped out of it, he suddenly realized that Stark was right about his emotional state. His mood swings were roller-coaster rides, and there wasn't anything he could do to stop it.

He entered his room, closed the door, and was about to phone Stark, when the phone rang. He picked it up, and said, "Boxer here."

"Kate here," the voice on the other end said.

"Okay, you're there, and I'm here. Now, that we've established that fact, what next?"

"My, my, aren't we testy this afternoon."

"Afternoons are my testy time," Boxer responded.

"I called, my darling, to let you know that I'll be there in a half-hour," Kate said.

"I can't wait."

"I hope you don't become too impatient and start without me," Kate said.

And before he could answer, she clicked off.

Boxer looked at the phone, shook his head, and put it down. Then he went to the window and looked out. From it, he could see the White House.

"The problem with you, Kate, is that you are too damn aggressive," he said out loud, and in a silent voice, he added, *And the problem with you, Jack, is that you're feeling more and more sorry for yourself.*

He turned from the window, went back to the phone, and punched out Stark's number. On the third ring, Stark picked it up.

"It's Jack," Boxer said.

"Mittenkope is off the deep end," Stark said.

"What?"

"We were out walking, and he ran in the water, shouting in German. I finally got him to come out, and he told me that the dead men — the sailors of all the ships he had sunk — are after him."

"That's just great. Where is he now?"

"Sleeping."

"Imagine what he's going to be like on the boat?"

"No thank you. You have your nightmares, and I have mine."

Boxer paced back and forth, limited by the length of the phone cord. "He must be with us to interpret the charts. The markings are his, and he has the Sixty-nine's log."

"Oh, he'll be with us, at least part of the time," Stark said.

"There must be something we can give him that will increase his lucidity."

"Remember me, I'm your former commanding officer, not your all-around doctor or even your psychiatrist."

"Yeah, tell me about it," Boxer said, then suddenly he had an idea and added, "Bring him up to Bethesda... I'll clear it with Pierce."

"What time?"

"Around eleven hundred."

"See you then," Stark said.

Boxer put the phone down. What he didn't need was a problem, not when he was trying to come to grips with *his* problems. But that was the way it had always been. He never had much time for himself.

He picked up the phone again and punched out Pierce's number.

His secretary came on and told him that Pierce was in conference.

"Have him call Admiral Boxer as soon as he can. He has the number," Boxer replied.

"Yes, sir," the secretary responded.

Boxer replaced the phone in its cradle, slipped off his shoes, removed his shirt, and dropped down on the bed. The prospect of going back to sea again in a submarine neither pleased or displeased him, and it was this neutrality of feeling that bothered him. He was, by nature, a man who had strong feelings about things, one way or another. Perhaps —

The sound of a key in the lock stopped his thoughts, and he looked at the door.

Suddenly, he heard Kate say, "What are you doing?" Then she shouted, "Take your hands off of me!"

Boxer was up on his feet, grabbed the .38, and went to the door.

Kate shouted, "Let me go! Let me go! Jack —"

Boxer flung the door open.

One of the men saw Boxer, yelled something in Chinese, and started to raise his .357.

"Mistake, mister," Boxer said, and squeezed off two rounds. Two pops sounded almost simultaneously.

The man fell to his knees, then forward.

Kate was still struggling with the other man.

"That's it!" Boxer yelled. "Freeze."

The man tried to grab Kate and use her for a shield.

She kneed him in the groin and broke away.

The man doubled up, sank to the floor, and tried to crawl away.

Boxer grabbed hold of him, pulled him to his feet, and threw him against the wall.

"Call the police, Kate, while I frisk the son-of-a-bitch," Boxer said. He looked at her. She was frozen with fear. "Go ahead, call them. You're okay, now."

She nodded and disappeared into the room.

"You're clean," Boxer said. "Just don't make a move, or you'll lose your balls." Boxer went over to the man he'd shot. He was on the floor, face down. He used his foot to roll him over. "He bought it," he said.

The man gave no indication that he'd heard him.

Kate came out of the room. "They're on their way here," she said in a whisper.

Boxer nodded, and with a slight smile playing on his lips, he said, "You sure do get yourself into a lot of trouble." He gestured toward the dead man. "You even got yourself a corpse."

"Corpse?"

Boxer nodded. "Corpse, like dead!"

"Oh my God!"

"If you're going to faint, do it inside the room near the bed," Boxer said.

"You're a bastard!" Kate exclaimed.

"No," he said quietly. "I'm just used to playing hardball, and you, my dear, mistakenly believe that you can. Or, to put it another way, maybe you can play hardball, but the losers don't wind up dead."

Kate didn't answer.

CHAPTER 12

Fong Shun Un and Shmuh Geh Gee were seated in Luk Shen Koo Gul's office. Each of the brothers sat in a high-backed, thickly stuffed black leather chair. They had arrived two hours before from JFK and were anxious to find out what Luk Shen was doing to get the charts. It was now eight-thirty at night, and each of the brothers could see the yellow streetlight outside glowing dimly through the dirty window.

"We have a problem," Luk Shen Koo Gul said in Cantonese, as he smoked a very large cigar.

"I don't like problems," Fong Shun Un said. He turned to his brother. "Do you like problems?"

"Never saw a problem I like," Shmuh Geh Gee answered.

Luk Shen took the cigar out of his mouth and moved his eyes to the left and to the right to make sure his bodyguards were in the right places. Then he said, "Through some mix-up my best man, Hok Chen, was busted by the police, and another of my men, not so good as Hok Chen, is now in the morgue, and I will have to support his family for the rest of my life. I do that for the families of the men who get wasted on the job. I mean, they don't have any union or medical coverage. I do what's right, right?"

Fong Shun Un waved his hand, indicating that he wasn't in the least bit interested in Luk Shen's labor relations, good or bad. "I think you're trying to tell me something that I don't want to hear."

Luk Shen explained what happened.

Fong Shun Un listened, nodded, and when Luk Shen Koo Gul was finished, he said, "Your best man wasn't good enough." Then looking at his brother, he said, "Deal's off, we go." He stood up.

Shmuh Geh Gee stood up.

"You can't just say the deal is off and walk out of here, leaving me with one of my men in the hands of the cops and another dead," Luk Shen said.

"Deal's off," Fong Shun Un said, suddenly flicking a knife out from the right sleeve of his jacket and hurling it at Luk Shen.

The blade thudded into Luk Shen's chest. He dropped his cigar and tried to pull the knife out.

Fong Shun Un's hand went to his 9mm, which he pointed at one of the bodyguards, while Shmuh Geh Gee covered the other. Fong Shun Un said, "My brother, Shmuh Geh Gee, is your new boss. He takes over everything. Now you work for him, and he works for me. Pass the word. Anyone complains, tell him to come see me. Understand?"

Both men swore on the graves of their ancestors that they understood.

"Also pass the word that from now on there isn't any handout to the families of the men who get killed or busted on the job. They want money, they have to work. The sons work for me. The mother and daughters, they work on the street, or, if they're very pretty, in whorehouse."

He went over to the desk and looked at Luk Shen Koo Gul. "He's still alive," he said as he put the muzzle of his gun against the back of the man's head. "Now, he's dead." He squeezed off a round. "Now get this body out of here and send someone in to clean up the blood."

"I'm hungry," Shmuh Geh Gee complained.

"Me too," Fong Shun Un responded and, pointing to one of the bodyguards with his gun, he said, "Take me to one of the restaurants I own."

"Sure, boss," the man answered. "Sure!"

"That was absolutely fabulous cooking," Boxer said, complimenting Tanya on the roast leg of lamb and roast veal she'd prepared for dinner. He was sitting to Borodine's right at the dinner table. Tanya was at the foot of the table. Kate sat next to him, and Ilia faced them.

"Absolutely," Kate chimed in.

Tanya blushed and thanked them. "I can't take all the credit. Ilia did the veal."

Boxer smiled, turned toward her, and, raising the small vodka glass in front of him, he said, "I salute the two of you." And as he tossed down the vodka, he was aware that the woman's blue eyes locked with his. She wasn't nearly as beautiful as Kate, but there was something about her — a kind of inner smoldering — that was very attractive. She was almost as tall as he, had a very curvaceous body, and a lovely face that needed very little makeup. And yet, the simple green dress she wore made her seem almost drab looking by comparison to Kate, who wore a gold lamé sheath that highlighted every curve of her body.

"Well, Doctor, I can see that you are a woman of many talents," Kate said.

Boxer was aware of the cat's claws in that remark, and, dropping his right hand below the level of the table, he squeezed Kate's knee.

"Tell me, do you have other talents besides cooking and —"

"I paint and I do some writing," Ilia answered.

"Don't let her get away with that," Tanya said, "She's had several of her stories and poems published, and two of her paintings have taken first prizes in —"

"Oh, I write too," Kate said. "But painting is out of my line."

"Kate writes professionally," Boxer said. "She's a journalist."

Ilia nodded and said, "That's well beyond my ability. I'm an amateur, nothing more."

"Oh, I'm sure you're not an amateur at anything that you decide to do," Kate replied.

Those cat's claws were out again, and Boxer squeezed Kate's knee again, much harder than he had a few moments before.

"Will you please excuse me," Tanya said. "I must get the dessert, and cake... Ilia baked the cake."

"I'll help," Ilia offered.

"No, no," Tanya said. "I can manage." And she left the table, calling to Borodine to follow her.

"Now you know who really has the rank in this family," Borodine said as he made a slight bow and left the table.

Kate focused her attention on Ilia and asked, "When will you be going back to Russia?"

"I imagine after I finish my latest assignment," Ilia answered.

"Oh, and what is that?"

"I am to be the ship's doctor for a salvage operation," Ilia answered.

"What?" Kate questioned, her cheeks suddenly scarlet. "What salvage operation?"

Ilia shrugged, looked straight at Boxer and said, "Comrade Admiral, perhaps you should explain. I know nothing about the actual operation."

Boxer rubbed his hand over his chin. He didn't appreciate the position in which he suddenly found himself.

"Well, Jack?" Kate questioned.

"It's a joint U.S. and Soviet operation. That's about all I want to tell you."

"And that's why someone wanted to kill you and tried to kidnap me?"

Ilia's blue eyes opened wide. "Someone tried —"

Tanya returned with a tray on which lay slices of cake and an assortment of cookies.

"It's called hardball," Kate said. "Only the person who told me that didn't bother to tell me what the game was really about."

Ilia looked confused.

"Ah, bobka!" Boxer exclaimed, recognizing the cake.

"Well, are you going to tell me about the salvage operation?" Kate asked.

Borodine reentered the room, carrying another tray that had a carafe of coffee, a bowl of vanilla ice cream, and a bowl of whipped cream.

"No," Boxer said quietly. "Any word that gets out about it will make the job that much more risky."

Borodine added, "There are people who would —"

"They already tried to kill Jack and kidnap me," Kate said. "I think I should at least know why."

"Greed," Boxer answered.

Borodine echoed the word.

"That doesn't tell me a hell of a lot," Kate complained.

"I'll make you a promise, if we get what we are after, then you'll have first dibs on the story," Boxer said.

"Is that a real promise or just words to keep me from harassing you?"

"There are witnesses here," Boxer answered.

"First crack?" Kate said again.

"First crack," Boxer answered.

"Now that you two have settled that, let's enjoy the dessert," Borodine said.

"I'll start with the bobka," Boxer said.

"Now, how did I know you'd start with that?" Kate commented. Then she said, answering her own question, "I guess I'm just psychic."

"No, but you are a cat," Boxer whispered under his breath.

"And you're just an ol' hound dog sniffing around, aren't you?" she responded.

"Coffee?" Boxer said with a smile.

Neither Boxer nor Kate spoke much during the ride back to the hotel.

Boxer knew he was sinking into one of his gray moods, but he really didn't have anything he wanted to chat about. He also was sure that Kate was more than slightly angry with him, though that didn't really bother him.

He checked the desk for messages. There was one from Stark telling him that "Things were back to normal." That meant, of course, Captain Mittenkope had returned to the present.

When they reached the door of Boxer's room, Kate asked in a voice dripping with sarcasm, "Are you sure that you want me in your bed tonight, or would you rather be left alone to dream about what it would be like to screw Ilia?"

"The choice is yours," Boxer answered, opening the door. He was not pleased with her attitude, and as he waited off to the side for a moment, he asked, "In or out?"

Passing him, Kate walked into the room.

Boxer closed the door and locked it.

"I'm so angry at you, I could —"

"You were acting —"

"I wasn't acting," she answered peevishly. "I was protecting—"

"I don't need your protection," Boxer said, taking off his jacket and hanging it in the closet. "I can take care of myself."

"Against guys with guns, but not against a gal who has the hots for you," Kate said.

Boxer unknotted his tie.

"Listen, I saw all the signs," Kate told him.

Boxer shook his head.

"What's that supposed to mean?" Kate asked, then, before he could answer, she said, "Just because you've been a cocksman all of your life that doesn't mean you're an expert about women."

"Why don't you undress, and we'll shower together," Boxer suggested. "I really don't want to get into a dog-and-cat fight with you, Kate."

She stalked over to the other side of the room and dropped her evening bag on the dresser. Then, kicking off her shoes, she said, "Unzip me."

Boxer obliged, and the sheath slipped off her body, leaving her naked except for a pair of white bikini panties, which she quickly removed.

"You could have told me about the salvage —"

"Why?" Boxer asked. He was standing close to her. Naked, she was really beautiful. "What we share has nothing to do with what I do," he told her.

Putting her hands on her hips and looking at him defiantly, she told him, "It does when I was almost kidnapped because of it."

Boxer shrugged. "The *almosts* are like the *ifs* in life, they don't really count," he said. Then, he stepped back and removed the rest of his clothing.

"That Russian woman knew," Kate said.

"Only that it was a salvage operation," Boxer said, heading for the bathroom. "Besides, she had to know that. There are certain aspects of medicine that she would have to bone up on."

Kate followed him. "She's going to be aboard the ship the whole time, isn't she?"

Boxer was about to say "Boat, not ship," but he stopped himself. Instead, he asked, "How do you like the water — hot, cool, or tepid?"

"Hot."

"Good, so do I," he said, adjusting the flow of the water. When he was satisfied, he glanced at Kate, smiled, and beckoned her with his finger.

She preceded him into the shower.

Boxer stepped into the narrow confines of the stall and immediately pulled her wet body against his.

"You think all you have to do is cock your finger at me, and I'll come running," Kate pouted.

Boxer reached for the soap and began soaping her breasts.

"Your problem is —"

"What's my problem?" he asked.

"I can't think straight when you're playing with me."

"Good, then maybe you'll stop jabbering about nonsense, and we can get down to more serious things," Boxer said as he turned her toward him and kissed her hard on her lips.

Putting her arms around his neck, she opened her mouth and gave him her tongue.

"I think we better get out of here," Boxer said.

"I think we better get the soap off before we do," she answered, smiling at him.

Moments later they were out of the shower and vigorously toweling one another.

"I'm not just sleeping with you," Kate said as they went toward the bed hand in hand. "I'm in love with you."

Boxer swept her into his arms and carried her the remaining few feet to the bed, where he gently set her down.

"Don't you love me, even a little bit?" Kate asked plaintively.

Boxer hovered over her naked body. He wanted very much to tell her what she wanted to hear, but he couldn't. He enjoyed her; he liked being with her, but he couldn't honestly say that he loved her.

"This isn't the time or the place to ask that, is it?" Kate said.

Boxer settled next to her. "It's okay, I understand. But I don't want to lie to you, Kate. I like having you here with me, and I like being with you. For now, at least, that's all I can give you, tell you... I know it's not what you need or what you want to hear."

After a long silence, she answered in a small voice, "I guess if I'm not willing to settle for that, then I should leave." She took a deep breath, slowly exhaled, and said, "I'm not willing to do that either." And turning to him, she whispered, "Make love to me, Jack... Make love to me!"

CHAPTER 13

Two days later Boxer drove down to Norfolk to take command of the boat, SSN-1S. The day was delightfully warm, and the sky was very blue with bright sunshine.

The SSN-1S was at the far end of the base, near the area where the drydocks were located. Her sail was fully raised, and the trim planes on it were secured. A floating crane was lowering the Russian submersible onto the modified forward deck hatch, while on the deck yardmen were waiting to secure it to the hatch's coaming.

The boat was thirty thousand tons of steel, ceramic sheathing, and high-tech electronic devices for deepwater rescue and salvage operations.

There were two Marine guards manning the checkpoint to get on the pier. Farther on, about two hundred feet from the checkpoint, there were two more armed guards posted at the boat's gangway.

As soon as Boxer IDed himself to the Marines, they snapped to attention and saluted him. He returned the courtesy. The two guards at the boat's gangway saluted him, but not with the same snap that the Marines had.

Boxer went aboard, turned to the stern, saluted the flag, then said to the Deck Officer, "Admiral Boxer requests permission to come aboard."

"Permission granted," the man answered, whom Boxer immediately recognized as Master Chief Paul Hanson. Hanson had been with him on his last two assignments.

The chief, a tall, rangy man from Kansas, said, "There're more than two dozen old-timers aboard, sir. All of the rates were with you a couple, three times before."

Boxer nodded. "Pass the word, I'll be around to welcome them. There'll be some new men on this assignment. Keep an eye on them, Chief."

"Yes, sir," Hanson answered.

"Any of the other officers aboard yet?" Boxer asked.

"Captain Paskudnyak and Dr. Ilia Ioff," Hanson answered.

Boxer nodded and proceeded to the door, which was secured open, at the forward part of the sail; then he stopped, turned, and asked, "Have any of our SEALS come aboard yet?"

"Karney and Melrose," Hanson answered. "They were with us the last time out."

"Have them arrange to have an underwater team in the water as soon as possible. I want a guard maintained until we shove off."

"Aye, aye, sir," Hanson answered. "I'll take care of it immediately."

Boxer entered the sail, looked up through a maze of wave guides, cables, and several differing kinds of antennae to where an open hatchway showed a round circle of blue sky. On either side of that open hatchway was the bridge. Fifteen feet down and forward of where the sail was housed when the boat ran underwater, lay the control room, which was his domain.

Boxer continued down the steel companionway to the fifteen-foot level, walked aft a dozen feet, and came to his cabin. He was about to open the door when a door across the passageway opened, and Paskudnyak boomed, "I was wondering when you were coming aboard, Admiral."

The two men beamed at one another and vigorously shook hands.

Paskudnyak was already in his dark green coveralls, the working uniform aboard any of the U.S.N.'s boats.

"I was just going to have a look-see," Paskudnyak said.

"If you wait until I change, I'll go with you," Boxer said. Paskudnyak was the boat's operational skipper, while he was the operation's commander. Their responsibilities were clearly defined, though in an emergency, if Boxer saw fit to override Paskudnyak's orders with commands of his own, he had the authority to do it.

"Thanks for pulling me off that attack boat," Paskudnyak said as he followed Boxer into his quarters. "Just like the room you had in Hong Kong," he laughed.

"Nothing like it," Boxer answered.

"Those hotel dudes wouldn't know what to do with a space this small, and these are the accommodations for an admiral, no less."

"No less," Boxer laughed. "This is what you can look forward to if you ever make flag rank."

"Hell, I'm not going to wait around to see if that happens," Paskudnyak said. "If we hit the jackpot, I'm going to take my share and buy a life without a care in the world."

"You show me where to buy that, and I will buy one too," Boxer said, stripping down to his underwear and going to the small metal closet where the coveralls were stored. He'd arranged to have his clothing sent aboard the previous day. All he came from D.C. with was a shoulder bag with his toilet articles.

"You know what I mean, Jack. I want something that will give me —"

"I know what you mean," Boxer interrupted. "I've been having similar thoughts myself. Maybe we'll have the opportunity to compare notes."

Paskudnyak nodded.

Boxer zipped up his coveralls and said, "Let's take that look-see."

"When is the U-boat ace coming aboard?" Paskudnyak asked.

"Sometime later today. He's coming up with Stark."

"A more unlikely duo I couldn't imagine," Paskudnyak commented.

They entered the control room.

"What you see is a marvel of modern technology," Paskudnyak said.

Boxer had studied the layout of the control room from the boat's plans the day before in Kahn's office. The boat was fully automated. All operations were controlled from the control room and were located on a single console. These operations included the firing of any weapon from the boat. In the event of a main system failure, there were backup systems for the diving, fire control, damage control, and engineering.

But the most obvious improvement was the large screen UWIS — Under Water Imaging System — which now gave the boat's skipper a three-dimensional view of his targets at maximum range of twenty thousand yards and a minimum of ten. It could also acquire and track incoming torpedoes, indicate evasive action, and assign defensive weaponry to counter the torpedoes. For the boat's skipper, it was the equivalent of the fighter pilot's head's up display.

"Well, at least I'll have a throne this trip out," Paskudnyak said, pointing to the elaborate captain's chair in front of the control console. Each arm of the chair was equipped with push buttons that would enable Paskudnyak to have instant communication with any of the boat's section chiefs, any of the submersibles, and Navy HQ in Washington, via satellite or through the special Navy radio facility in Michigan.

"You sit, while I have to stand in the CR or keep to my cubbyhole," Boxer complained.

Paskudnyak grinned. "So you finally realized that though rank has its privileges, high rank loses some of them. And — Don't turn around, but unless I've become very, very ill, one of the loveliest women I have ever seen has just entered the CR."

Boxer looked over his right shoulder and said, "Welcome to the CR, Comrade Doctor Ioff. This is Captain Paskudnyak, the boat's skipper."

Paskudnyak gulped, managed a smile and whispered to Boxer, "I think I'm in love, Jack."

Boxer glanced at him.

"I know I am," Paskudnyak whispered.

"A pleasure to meet you, Comrade Captain," Dr. Ioff said, extending her hand.

Paskudnyak gently took hold of it, and with almost courtly charm, he said, "The pleasure is all mine," then he kissed the back of it.

Boxer was too surprised to react, and when he did, he could only say, "The comrade doctor is an internist."

"Ah yes, I would have guessed that," Paskudnyak replied, his tone tinged with mystery.

"I did not mean to interrupt you, but I was attempting to familiarize myself with sections of the boat," Ioff explained.

"No explanation needed," Paskudnyak answered. "Please, feel free to come to the CR —"

"What is the CR?" she asked, looking at Boxer.

"The control room," Paskudnyak answered, then turning to Boxer, he said, "If we're finished here, sir, I will take the doctor on a tour of the boat."

"We're finished," Boxer answered, hardly able to keep himself from laughing. Paskudnyak was, if anything, a more notorious cocksman than he, and certainly had a love 'em and leave 'em attitude.

"If you will excuse me, I will go with the captain," the doctor said.

"Certainly," Boxer answered.

By 1600 that day, the entire complement was aboard, and Paskudnyak ordered the crew to make ready to get under way.

At 1630, with Paskudnyak at the conn on the bridge, Boxer alongside of him, and Borodine below in the CR to monitor the system status next, she eased into mid-channel at "slow, ahead," and made a starb'd turn, heading down the Chesapeake toward the ocean.

"We'll dive once we're past the two-mile limit," Paskudnyak said.

"She's your boat," Boxer answered. "I'm just here for the ride."

"You're never on any boat 'just for the ride,'" Paskudnyak answered.

Surface radar began to report targets.

Paskudnyak contacted the RO and told him to keep his reports to those targets that came within a thousand yards of the boat.

The famous Chesapeake Bay Bridge grew larger and larger as they drew closer to it.

"I guess I'm never really sorry to leave," Boxer said, looking toward the shore where the beach houses were clearly visible.

"That's why you're a sailor man," Paskudnyak answered. "Why I am one too."

Boxer accepted the answer without comment. Each leaving, as far as he was concerned, was always a kind of entering, a kind of beginning, and no two of them were ever alike.

An amber signal light began to flash on the bridge control console.

"Radio room, sir," one of the two rates on the bridge said.

"Captain here," Paskudnyak said into the headset phone in front of him.

"Alert message from HQ," the communications officer said.

"Read it."

"'Have good reason to believe bandits have Libyan connection and have the use of a sophisticated sub capable of affecting salvage operation in deep water. Also capable of launching offensive and defensive weapons against other undersea craft.' Signed Kahn. That's it, sir."

Paskudnyak thanked the COMMO and said to Boxer, "We have trouble." He explained the content of the message.

"You really didn't expect Fong Shun Un and Shmuh Geh Gee to walk away from this. Christ, they had someone try to blow me away and kidnap Kate. They want what we want, and they will kill us to get it."

"Yeah, I know. But I was sure as hell hoping that it wouldn't come to that."

"I'm not much of a hoper in matters like that," Boxer said. "I'm not much of a hoper about anything, when you get right down to it."

Paskudnyak gave him a peculiar look.

Boxer smiled and shrugged, somewhat surprised that he had revealed something so private.

Paskudnyak increased the speed to one-third ahead, and within less than twenty minutes they passed under Chesapeake

Bridge. Almost immediately the boat reacted to the swell of the ocean.

"All hands... All hands, this is the captain. All hands... All hands diving stations... Stand by for a manual dive. Repeat, this is a manual dive... All hands, stand by to dive," Paskudnyak announced over the 1MC. He pushed the klaxon button, holding it for a long blast. Then over the 1MC, he called out, "Dive... Dive..."

Boxer went down the hatch first, Paskudnyak followed. The last rate pulled the hatch down and dogged it shut.

Paskudnyak sat on the captain's chair and into his mike, he said to the diving officer, "Make two hundred."

"Aye, aye, sir, making two hundred," the DO repeated.

Instantly, there was the hiss of escaping air as the ballast tanks were being opened and the status control board showed that diving planes were angled down five degrees for the dive.

Boxer watched the red digital readout of the depth gauge, as the numbers flicked by.

In minutes the boat was below a hundred feet, and its bow was still angled down.

The diving planes were repositioned to their horizontal mode, and the boat shifted slightly up, but it was still heading down.

The sound of the ballast pumps filled the boat as the DO ordered the water vented from its tanks. The boat's descent slowed. The digital readout indicated she was going below two hundred. The hiss of air filled the boat as high-pressure air was fed into the ballast tanks. The boat was down to 225, then she began to rise.

"Mark, two hundred," the DO announced as the boat stabilized at the required depth.

"Well done," Boxer said, knowing just how difficult it was to bring a boat to a specific depth and hold it there. Making a boat dive or surface was much like making a blimp gain or lose altitude; the difference between them was dictated by the specific medium in which they operated.

Paskudnyak passed the words of praise to the DO, then he called for a course change that headed the boat into the South Atlantic for its brief shakedown cruise.

Captain Zaynad stood alongside Fong Shun Un and pointed to the bright spot on the sonar display scope and said, "That's your boat."

"Can they see us?"

"Maybe yes, maybe no. But they won't do anything until we do," Zaynad said confidently.

"Why won't they —"

With a shrug, Zaynad said, "Americans are impossible to figure out."

"This one sly," Fong Shun Un commented. "He play by his rules, only."

Zaynad nodded. "Years back when I was a younger officer, he sank the boat I was on. Only myself and three other men escaped."

"This time we kill 'im," Fong Shun Un said. "I sink the bastard," he suddenly shouted, breaking the silence of the CR.

Zaynad ignored the outburst and explained, "We will follow, and when the time comes we will strike and destroy them."

"We kill first, then take the gold," Fong Shun Un said. "We get the gold," he shouted. He wanted Zaynad to know that getting the gold was more important than destroying Boxer. He'd boarded the submarine from a yacht the previous night, and already he felt that Zaynad, because he wore a uniform, was going to try to outrank him.

In the face of Fong Shun Un's outburst, Zaynad remained calm. "Certainly, my orders include the salvaging of the gold, but that will not be able to be done until —"

"Fuck orders, my orders important now. Understan'? *My* orders," Fong Shun Un said in a booming voice. Then, he smiled. "I make every man millionaire; that's what I do."

"If the SO says something is out there," Paskudnyak said, "then you can make book on it that something is out there, even though it doesn't show on the UWIS."

Boxer, Borodine, Stark, and Mittenkope stood in front of the large sonar display scope, while the SO, Lt. Jessy Juarez, a short, dark-complexioned man who had just finished giving them a detailed description of the ghost target, stood to one side.

"And you are sure that it is not a marine creature?" Stark asked.

"Sir, I have no idea what it is. But whatever it is, it has been following us from the day we left our shake-down area."

"It never comes within range of our gear?" Boxer asked.

"Never, sir. That's why the men have dubbed it the 'ghost target'."

"It has to be my sons," Mittenkope said with obvious pride in his voice.

"Listen, Captain, if it is them, and they come anywhere near us, I'm going to blow them the fuck out of the water," Paskudnyak said.

"Ah, but they will have died gloriously!" Mittenkope said, adding, "And in a submarine too."

Paskudnyak rolled his eyes, but didn't say anything more.

Boxer rubbed his chin, knowing that, whoever it was, they weren't there to play games; they were there for the same reason that he was, and he was certain the only *they* who it could possibly be would be Fong Shun Un, Shmuh Geh Gee and — the *and* wasn't a whole hell of a lot important.

"Are you thinking what I think you're thinking?" Borodine asked.

"And how would I know what you're thinking?" Boxer answered, absolutely sure that their thoughts were the same. Professionally, they thought exactly alike, and once they were even in love with the same woman. But they were really very different men. Boxer recognized that Borodine was a chess player while he, himself, preferred poker, and was considered by many to be a shade less expert than a professional gambler.

"Skip the few days shore time, and head straight for our goal," Borodine said.

"Right again," Boxer exclaimed, then looking at Paskudnyak, he gave the necessary verbal orders, including one to notify Langley and tell them the change of plans, but not the reason for the change.

"Kahn doesn't like changes," Stark commented. "He's a bureaucrat right down to his brain cells."

"That's where it all starts — the love of paperwork, meetings, and things like that," Boxer responded, smiling.

"You can't kid me," Paskudnyak added. "It's really congenital. Something went wrong with the man's DNA."

Boxer nodded. "You might be right, but it's our responsibility to let him know when we change our plans."

"Just once, I'd like him to come on a mission with us."

"Never happen. His kind are deck birds," Stark said. "And if you look at it from a realistic point of view, we certainly need those kinds of individuals too."

"I don't," Paskudnyak said, and before anyone could make another comment, he added, "If you will excuse me, I have a few things that require my immediate attention."

"You're excused," Boxer said, and, turning to Borodine, he asked, "How about a cup of coffee and a piece of good old American apple pie. I understand the baker is an artist with pies, cheesecake and breads."

"Sounds good to me," Borodine answered.

Boxer was amazed at how quickly Borodine had managed to pick up Americanisms and include them in his speech.

The two men walked aft and entered the wardroom. Both served themselves coffee, and Boxer cut two wedges from a fresh apple pie that was still hot enough to steam when he inserted the knife into the top of the crust.

They sat opposite each other at a small table.

"How are your men getting on?" Boxer asked.

"*Glasnost* is in full swing," Borodine answered.

"Good!"

"Any complaints from your side?" Borodine asked.

"None."

"Good," Borodine answered, then he said, "Jack —"

"Ah, when you use my Christian name, I know something is wrong."

Borodine placed the coffee mug on the table, and, looking straight at Boxer, he said, "Something is different about you. I can't exactly put my finger on it, but there is something different."

"What you see is what I am. Isn't that the expression?" Boxer answered.

Borodine looked straight into Boxer's eyes. "What I see is a man who is at war with himself, a man who, as you Americans say, is 'running on empty.'"

"Maybe running on full," Boxer answered.

Borodine remained silent for several moments, then in an almost inaudible whisper, he said, "I think I know what you mean."

"I'll work it out," Boxer told him cheerily. "I'm like the proverbial cat: I always come up on my feet."

Borodine smiled. "We're two of a kind," he responded.

"Not to change the subject, but to change it to something more interesting: how is the good doctor doing?" Boxer asked.

"Well, I imagine. I only see her at mess, and then she doesn't spend much time there. Captain Paskudnyak, I noticed, is very attentive to her."

"He's got a thing about beautiful women," Boxer said with a laugh, because he knew exactly what Borodine's response would be.

"That's a little like the kettle calling the pot black, isn't it?"

"I knew you would say something like that," Boxer replied.

"Well, isn't it?"

Boxer nodded.

"Have you mentioned anything to him about Ilia's emotional state?" Borodine asked.

"No. After all, Igor, I only command this operation in conjunction with you, and neither of us is expected to be the father to our subordinates."

Borodine agreed with a nod, but then he said, "Nonetheless, one of us should at least mention it to him. She is a member of the crew, and we are responsible for her well-being."

"Igor, her personal life is her personal life. She owns it, and no one has the right to interfere," Boxer said.

"Let's not call it interference; let's call it intervention."

"Is there a difference?"

"Semantically, perhaps... But for our purpose, only the end matters. Will you speak to him?"

"Only tangentially," Boxer said. "I am not the man to advise another man on their emotional involvement with women."

"On the contrary, your experience in that area makes you the perfect individual," Borodine said, draining the last bit of coffee from the mug. "If the Comrade Captain would weigh anyone's words, he'd weigh yours, and, I am sure, he would not find them wanting."

"Only tangentially," Boxer repeated.

Borodine smiled and said, "Maybe we missed our calling. Maybe we should have become priests. After all, we —"

Boxer guffawed.

Borodine started to laugh too.

The two of them laughed until tears came to their eyes and their sides hurt.

"Priests," Boxer repeated, still sputtering with laughter. "Priests!" And he started to guffaw again.

CHAPTER 14

The SSN-S1 reached the position marked on Mittenkope's charts four days after it finished its shakedown cruise. The ghost target came up on the sonar screen only to vanish before any kind of a fix on it could be obtained.

During the voyage to the salvage site, life aboard the boat was routine. Whatever problems occurred were taken care of by Paskudnyak, leaving Boxer the time he needed to study the plans of the *Edinburgh* and evolve a plan of ingress and egress, depending upon how she was settled on the bottom.

The gold was in a storage area amidship, four levels down. If the area was intact after the torpedo explosion, it would be easier to remove the gold than if the storage area had been badly damaged and the gold had dropped into the lower levels of the hull, or, still worse, if the gold actually went to the bottom, either as a result of the explosions or as a result of corrosion over the fifty years that the ship lay on the bottom. None of this, however, would be known until they actually surveyed the ship and had hard photographic evidence of her condition.

Boxer met with the American and Russian diving teams and went over their equipment with each group. Borodine was with him during these sessions.

Each diver had an individual diving pack which consisted of an ionic oxygen remover that removed dissolved oxygen in seawater of depths up to two thousand feet, and an emergency supply of a mixture of oxygen and helium that would last up to an hour, which would be more than enough time for the diver to come to the surface or enter one of the two submersibles that would be nearby. Each team had laser-cutting devices, and special robotic devices for transporting the gold from the interior of the vessel to the SSN-1S, which would take a position either on the bottom, close to the wreck, or remain stationary about fifty feet above it. And each member of the team was armed with a standard Marine-issue K-Bar knife, and a small but highly effective laser rifle.

The two American submersibles would be used to transport the divers to and from the wreck, while the Soviet craft would remain available for rescue work. The two transporters would be armed.

Boxer had several meetings with Ilia about the operation of the decompression chambers — there were three aboard: One large enough to hold ten men and the other two half that number.

Their meetings were always held either with Borodine or Stark present, and they were totally professional. Boxer, though aware of her attractiveness, never allowed it to become anything more than an objective observation. And though he did mention her emotional fragility to Paskudnyak, he did not make an issue of it.

Finally, on the morning that Boxer intended to send one of the submersibles to video the wreck, Mittenkope came to the bridge dressed in his old uniform.

"Periscope depth," he ordered.

Paskudnyak glanced at Boxer and said, "Give the son-of-a-bitch a boot in the ass and get him the hell out of here."

"Periscope depth, *Herr Kapitän*," Mittenkope said, using a different voice.

"Christ, he's playing all the parts now!" Paskudnyak exclaimed. "I've got a submersible to launch and he's playing kookoo games."

Boxer turned to one of the sailors and said, "Get a broomstick and give it to Captain Mittenkope."

"Aye, aye, sir," the man replied.

Boxer turned to Paskudnyak. "Begin launch procedure."

Paskudnyak announced over the 1MC, "All hands, this is the captain speaking. All hands, stand by to begin launch procedure." Then he dialed in 1200 rpms — just enough speed to hold steerage way.

"Steady, as she goes," he told the helmsman.

"Steady, as she goes," the rate repeated.

"Submersible one, prepare for launch," Paskudnyak said.

"All systems go," came over the PA.

"Flood launch bay one," Paskudnyak ordered.

"Flooding launch bay one," Master Chief Hanson reported.

Boxer scanned the systems status net. All of the boat's systems were green.

Paskudnyak ordered the bay doors open.

"Number one bay doors open," Hanson said.

"Stand by for launch," Paskudnyak said.

"Launch system green," Hanson reported.

"Ten seconds to launch," Paskudnyak said.

Boxer watched the launch clock's digital display.

"Eight, nine, mark!" Hanson said.

Paskudnyak pressed the red launch button on the control console.

On the TV monitor, a huge air bubble appeared behind the submersible, and the next instant it burst, and the craft was hurtling out of the boat. For the next few moments there wasn't any visual contact, though the craft's pilot, Lt. Peter

Harris, reported, "Launch successful, switching to on-board power."

"Roger that," Paskudnyak answered. He was in direct radio contact with the craft.

"On-board power green, extending wings," Harris said.

Then suddenly, the submersible came up on the UWIS. It looked like a giant stingray.

"Come to course one-four-zero," Paskudnyak said, after placing the wreck on the UWIS.

"Course one-four-zero," Harris said. "Speed six knots. High-intensity lights on. Video cameras on."

Boxer focused his attention to a video screen on the far right side of the control console, where a rate was adjusting the controls.

Slowly, out of the darkness ahead of the submersible's high-intensity lights, the wreck of the *Edinburgh* came into view. She was lying on her side, split amidship.

The closer the submersible went, the sharper the picture became.

Boxer moved closer to Paskudnyak. "Seems as if we hit it lucky. The gold is exposed — fourth level down, on the right-hand side."

"Harris, send robot out to examine fourth level, center, on the right-hand side," Paskudnyak said.

"Aye, aye, sir," Harris answered.

Suddenly Mittenkope shouted, "Everyone, this is Captain Mittenkope, I now have command of this boat. Our duty is to the Fatherland."

"He's got a fucking Luger in his hand," Paskudnyak said.

"The boat is —"

"Ah shit!" Paskudnyak exclaimed and launched himself at Mittenkope.

Even as Boxer rushed at Mittenkope, two quick explosions boomed in the control room.

Paskudnyak was flung back and crashed down on the deck.

Boxer smashed into Mittenkope, wrested the gun from his hand, and used it to cold cock him.

Hanson hunkered down next to Paskudnyak, felt for a pulse, and shaking his head, he said, "The skipper is dead."

Boxer went to the control console and over 1MC said, "Dr. Ioff report to the CR, on the double... Dr. Ioff report to the CR, on the double!"

"Robotic images on screen," one of the junior officers in the CR announced.

"Comrade Admiral Borodine, have Paskudnyak's body removed and make sure Mittenkope is attended to."

Boxer gave his attention to the screen where the interior of the cruiser was now displayed. Part of the gold bullion was clearly visible. The gold ingots, the size of bricks, were stacked from the floor to the ceiling.

Boxer opened the channel to the submersible. "Do a three-sixty, then return to base," he told Harris.

"Roger that," Harris answered.

Boxer switched off and turned his attention to Ilia, who was giving directions to several corpsmen. For a moment, she glanced up at him. Their eyes locked, but even before he could shake his head or speak, she broke the connection.

Boxer looked at the screen. The submersible was on the far side of the wreck, out of sight.

Stark came up to Boxer and said, "I didn't know he had a gun."

"Not your fault," Boxer answered.

"Nor yours," Stark said.

Boxer didn't answer.

"Why don't you turn the conn over to the XO," Stark suggested.

"As soon as we recover the submersible, I will," Boxer said. Then he added, "The salvage will be a piece of cake. All of the gold appears to be in the area where it had been stored."

Stark nodded.

Boxer looked up at the screen just in time to see the submersible turn into an orange ball. The thunderous roar of the explosion was immediately followed by a shock wave that violently shook the boat, knocking some of the men off their feet, and forcing Stark to grab onto the captain's chair for support.

Boxer opened the radio channel to the submersible, and called Harris.

The sound of static filled the CR.

"It's not going to be easy after all," Boxer said tightly. "It's going to mean a fight with Fong Shun Un and Shmuh Geh Gee." He switched on the 1MC, "All hands, now hear this... All hands, now hear this... This is Admiral Boxer. Captain Paskudnyak has been killed. I have taken over the command of SSN-1S. As of now, we are at battle stations. I repeat, we are at battle stations." Then he signaled "battle stations" on the klaxon.

Fong Shun Un saw the target disappear on the sonar display. "Gone... Pff, like smoke," he said, snapping his fingers.

Zaynad remained expressionless.

"You order attack other submarine," Fong Shun Un said.

Shmuh Gch Gee pushed the muzzle of a 9mm into Zaynad's right side. "Better do what Fong Shun Un say, or you dead meat," he said in a low voice.

Zaynad nodded slowly, and, pointing to the communications panel, he said, "I will order the torpedoes loaded."

"Only Captain move," Fong Shun Un said, waving the grenade he held so that everyone in the control could see it. He'd taken over the boat when he realized that Zaynad had no intentions of letting him command the operation.

Zaynad went to the communications panel, switched into the torpedo room, and in Arabic informed them what the situation in the control room was. He then said, "The only way we have a chance of getting out of this alive is to do what he wants us to. Maybe we'll get lucky and sink the American boat."

The Torpedo Officer answered, "Our best shots are the wire-guided torpedoes. We have four aboard. An attack with all of them and our Sea Darts might do it."

"Arm for that kind of attack," Zaynad responded.

"Aye, aye, Captain," the TO answered, then he added, "Allah is great!"

"Let's hope he's great enough to pull us out of this one," Zaynad said and switched off.

Boxer met with Borodine and Stark in the wardroom. They closed the door and sat at a table.

"That boat is on the other side of the wreck," Boxer said, "and it can remain there a long, long time. If we choose, we can outwait them. But that's not what I want to do."

"We risk being —" Stark began, and Boxer finished.

"Killed," he said. Then, before anyone else could speak, he said, "That's a risk I have taken many, many times before."

"What do you want to do, Jack?" Borodine asked.

"What they don't expect," Boxer said. "We blow the wreck apart — that is, where it's already split, we'll widen it even more — enough for us to pass through, and then we'll attack."

"That means we'll scatter the gold," Stark said.

Boxer shrugged. "If we make it, we can come back and pick the ingots up from the bottom... If we don't make it — well, at least we will have rid the world of Fong Shun Un and Shmuh Geh Gee."

"I don't want to be down here any longer than I have to," Borodine said.

Boxer looked at Stark.

"I'm not too old to still want some excitement in my life," Stark answered.

"Thank you, gentlemen," Boxer said, and, pointing to the coffee urn, he suggested they have coffee. Then he left the table, opened the door, and headed directly to the control room, where he opened the I1C, and said, "Juris, Pepe, and Alex report to the control room, on the double."

In less than two minutes the three men were standing in front of Boxer. It had been decided a week and a half before that the trio, instead of doing odd jobs, would work underwater. All of them had spent hours training with the special tanks. By now they were thoroughly familiar with the diving pack, the emergency equipment, and how to handle various kinds of underwater explosives.

"Time for the three of you to earn your pay," Boxer said. "You're going to go out, plant explosive charges in the wreck's hull, and blow it."

"Hey man, that's a piece of cake," Pepe said.

"It won't be if some other men try to stop you," Boxer said.

"Just let them try," Juris answered.

"As soon as you blow it, I'm going to take the boat through and attack the submarine that sank our submersible," Boxer explained.

"How do we get back on board?" Crespo asked.

"You don't. We won't be able to take you aboard. You head straight for the surface. There's a salvage ship up there. She'll take you aboard."

The three men looked at each other, and Juris said, "There's a chance that you guys won't make it, isn't there?"

"There's that chance," Boxer answered calmly. "Now get into your gear and head for the release chamber."

None of the three men moved.

"I gave you an order," Boxer told them.

Juris extended his hand and said, "See you, bro. Good luck."

Boxer shook each of their hands.

"Go with God," Pepe whispered as he walked away.

Boxer sat down in the captain's chair, switched on the communications systems, and, contacting the master diver, he said, "Stand by to open release chamber."

Within minutes the three divers were on the UWIS, heading toward the huge rent in the cruiser's hull.

Boxer signaled the salvage ship and told its captain to stand by to pick up three divers.

"What the hell is going on down there?" the skipper asked.

"Nothing that you can do anything about," Boxer answered, then he signed off and opened communications with Juris, Pepe, and Alex.

The men quickly became lost in the interior darkness of the hull. Boxer dared not turn on the boat's high-intensity lights for fear of revealing the divers. The only light they would have would come from a small lamp inside their diving helmets.

"Ten-minute fuse should give us time to clear it," Pepe told the other two.

"Seems right," Juris answered.

"Make it fifteen," Boxer said. "And that's an order."

"I forgot the man can hear us," Juris laughed.

"Man, it's dark down here," Alex said.

While they spoke, they planted Semtex in large globes on either side of the fracture and connected the necessary firing devices. The plastic explosives could be used underwater only with a special detonating shell that supplied ten seconds of oxygen.

After ten minutes, Juris reported, "All of the charges set and fused."

"Get out of there. Now," Boxer ordered.

"On our way," Juris answered.

Boxer ordered the boat's torpedoes and Sea Darts armed and loaded. Then he launched the second submersible, giving its pilot orders to attack from the starboard side at the same time that the SSN-1S came through the breach in the cruiser's hull.

Boxer watched the digital readout of the boat's master clock. "Five seconds," he reported over the 1MC. "Four seconds... Three seconds... Engine room flank speed... Two seconds..."

A huge explosion rocked the boat, and much of the wreck's hull was obliterated.

The SSN-1S pushed forward through the breach.

The explosion threw Fong Shun Un against the bulkhead. He dropped the grenade, tried desperately hard to recover it, but just as his fingers touched it, an explosion ripped open the control room, splitting the boat in half.

Boxer saw the boat break up on the UWIS and immediately ordered the speed reduced to "slow, ahead."

"That was from inside of her," Borodine said in a quiet voice.

Boxer took a deep breath, and as he slowly exhaled, he said, "I don't think there are any survivors, but we'll send a team to see anyway, then we'll go back and pick up the gold."

"You want me to take command now, Jack?" Borodine asked.

Boxer nodded. Then in a quiet voice he said, "I want to sleep for a very long time."

"Sleep as long as you want, old friend," Borodine answered.

Boxer left the captain's chair and walked slowly out of the control room. Maybe later, when he wasn't so tired, he'd go and speak with Ilia…

A NOTE TO THE READER

Dear Reader,

If you have enjoyed the novel enough to leave a review on **Amazon** and **Goodreads**, then we would be truly grateful.

Sapere Books

Sapere Books is an exciting new publisher of brilliant fiction and popular history.

To find out more about our latest releases and our monthly bargain books visit our website: **saperebooks.com**